# DR. WILLIAM HOBBYS

## THE PROMISCUOUS KING'S PROMISCUOUS DOCTOR

## PETER STRIDE

ISBN: 978-1-63950-283-7 (sc)
ISBN: 978-1-63950-287-5 (e)



Writers Apex

Gateway Towards Success

8063 MADISON AVE #1252
Indianapolis, IN 46227
+13176596889
www.writersapex.com

*Fiction can never atone for historical suffering*
—Rosemary Stride


*And in this seat of peace tumultuous wars*
*Shall kin with kin and kind with kind confound;*
*Disorder, horror, fear and mutiny*
*Shall here inhabit, and this land be call'd*
*The field of Golgotha and dead men's skulls.*
—Bishop of Carlisle



The life and death of Richard II Act 4, scene 1

# CONTENTS

# LONDON THE LATE TWENTY FIRST CENTURY

*ADULTEROUS PAST QUEENS OF ENGLAND invalidate current Royal Family's claim to the throne states DNA expert!* shouted the newspaper hoarding.

That was not what he said, trust the media to misunderstand science in favour of sensation. However if you dabble in genetic testing of persons of supposed royal blood, as with all people, there are going to be some surprises, clearly there had been several false paternities in the last half millennium, how unfair that these ladies, so discreet in their love affairs during their life time, should be found out by new science hundreds of years later. As the American novelist, Kurt Vonnegut said in 1976, history is merely a list of surprises, the advent of DNA testing had certainly made the surprises even larger in a way unimaginable only a few decades ago. However, he feared he may receive a Royal reprimand this morning.

The distinguished middle-aged gentleman with greying temples emerged in a charcoal suit and crested tie from the Roitt Institute of Genetics and Immunology, part of the new Middlesex Hospital, built in response to previously miscalculated community need, and following the damage caused to neighbouring hospitals by the London Cyclone. He reflected that the adverse effects of climate change could benefit some people. His chair as the Crick Professor of Genetics had been created for him when the Institute opened.

The old Middlesex Hospital had been demolished many decades earlier at the insistence of the bean counters in the National Health Department, supported by the Treasurer and the Cabinet. The only residual building left amid the high rise offices and big money apartments was the Middlesex Hospital Chapel, subsequently renamed the Fitzrovia and made into a licensed dance hall, largely, at a later date, as a front for a brothel. The only important paradigms of that period appeared to be the dollar earned immediately and celebrity status, the greed and label culture. Expert professionals were largely ignored, and preventative health programs that could save many dollars in the future were shelved. Decisions were made by anonymous economists who had little understanding of the virtues of the establishment, such as its history of research, high standards of clinical excellence, community service, and traditions dating back over two and a half centuries. The destruction of memory was of little account to government economists.

Little public support for such values was received at that time. The 'new-think' generation, a fortunately temporary but then vociferous loose coalition of self-professed neo-Marxists and Facebook warriors were determined to replace popular common-sense and tolerance with their own narrow extremism. They had a low opinion of authority, scientific knowledge and freedom of speech, unless it mirrored their left-wing beliefs, and had minimal respect for anything of traditional value. Passionate followers of screens of mutual ignorance, they saw little value in the old hospital.

An earnest young lady, the Doniach Fellow in the Institute, also in a charcoal suit, walked beside him towards the black Rolls Royce flying the Royal Standard for the short trip to Buckingham Palace, their relationship outwardly appearing entirely professional. Many of their colleagues thought they were courteous, but distant, even sometimes frosty. None, not even his unfaithful estranged wife, would have guessed that often, when working late in the DNA research laboratory after all their colleagues had left, she was an eager recipient of his DNA on the phlebotomy couch where volunteers donated blood samples to assist the research projects.

# BUCKINGHAM PALACE

The spotless gleaming black Rolls Royce, one of the new Silver Magna Cartas, turned out of the New Middlesex Hospital site on the corner of Regents Park, next to the Royal College of Physicians. This august body had been founded in 1518 in the time of unlamented Henry VIII, though, unlike its sister body, the Royal College of Surgeons, before he became the paranoid psychotic tyrant of his last decade. The luxurious vehicle purred down into the Portland Tunnel, emerged at the Hyde Park Corner exit, turned left into Constitution Hill, and through the front gates of Buckingham Palace.

They were rapidly ushered into the King's Study and the presence of the Monarch. The two doctors bowed their heads briefly while the sovereign extended a hand to shake with the guests. 'Welcome doctors, thank you for coming to see me when your work must keep you so busy. Dr Crick, I can't help myself looking at everyone's tie, you know my interest in heraldry, what does the shield on your tie represent?'

'Your Majesty, it shows three seaxes of the mid Saxons after whom Middlesex county is named, and three of the rod and serpent of Aesculapius to compliment the swords, it is the old Middlesex Hospital tie, and was the property of my maternal grandfather who was a consultant physician there.'

'Good to see a fine tradition still in use, so what surprise do you have for me, am I out of a job, Dr Crick, have you found someone with a more royal bloodline than mine?' the Sovereign inquired, with a faint hint of asperity. Dr Crick extracted two pages of notes from his brief case and handed them to the monarch.

'Your Majesty, I regret any offence caused to you by the press misquoting my research, the whole nation knows the most appropriate person sits on our throne, judged both by genetics and the love of your people. Medicine should reflect society with a blend of science and humanity, however those of us who work predominantly in the research laboratory get very absorbed in the science and the humanitarian aspects can be overlooked.

We have the results of the DNA studies on the bones in Westminster Abbey, which were purported to be those of the Princes in the Tower, Edward V and his brother Richard, Duke of York, the sons of Edward IV. Well the results for your eyes only initially are truly astonishing, perhaps it is as well you listened to those tiresomely persistent members of the Richard III Society. They certainly have established considerable credibility as experts on the history of that period. The discovery of Richard would not have happened without the enthusiasm of their members and especially the drive of Philippa Langley. The subsequent discovery of Richards skeletal remains under that car park at the previous site of Greyfriars Church and the identification of his remains was a unique piece of world class scholarship by the team from the University of Leicester. The discovery, and his reinterment in Leicester cathedral still generate enormous interest. It was most fortuitous that Richard's skeleton was found when it was as the direct female line, with matching mitochondrial DNA, has since become extinct, and it would be much harder to confirm that it was Richard. His supporters and detractors still seek the most accurate truth available, particularly about his two nephews.'

'Well, well..., how extraordinary. Forsooth, as Henry VI would have said.......Dr Crick, your skills match those of your most eminent great-grandfather who discovered this genetic material.' said the Monarch reading the report. 'Well, this astounding discovery blows previous theories, which had taken the gender of the bones for granted, out of the water; the reputation of Richard III appears at least partially restored, we will have to revise our knowledge and understanding of the history of that time. Perhaps Richard was not the villain portrayed by Shakespeare.'

Crick interjected, 'your majesty, many of my friends have thought Shakespeare's Richard III was so exaggerated and improbable as a portrayal of any human being, that the play must be seen as a comedy, with due respect to yourself, it was to mock the Tudors' sense of self-importance. Certainly the concept of Richard being in utero for two years, which originated with the writings of John Rous, failed to impress the Guinness Book of Records! Cecily Neville does not appear in the list of longest proven periods of gestation! Slowly English public opinion is moving to the view point that Henry VIII was a much more brutal villain than Richard III in spite of the BBC's affection for "bluff King Hal".'

The monarch continued, 'this poses more questions than it answers. At least this does not appear quite as scandalous as the false-paternity of the Beauforts!' The monarch turned to Dr. Crick's young colleague, with a smile to put her at ease. 'And Dr Hobbys-Pole, I understand you can trace your ancestors back on your side to a Yorkist royal physician, and to the Plantagenet's on your husband's side, how interesting, how eminent. Perhaps you should have my job!'

'Your Majesty,' said Dr Hobbys-Pole, 'my ancestors were Poles, descendants of the House of York, but I would much rather have my job than yours, you will not find me assembling an army for an insurrection to have a rerun of the Battle of Bosworth! Anyway Margaret Pole was the daughter of George of Clarence, brother to Edward IV and Richard III. Her claim to the throne disappeared with the act of attainder against George who was drowned in a butt of malmsey as legend relates! Henry VIII removed most of the Plantagenets who had a claim to the throne, predominantly once he developed the unfortunate and character changing tyrannical paranoid psychosis of McLeod's syndrome.

We are fortunate that the descendants of Richard and Edward's sister Anne of York went largely under his radar, otherwise that brilliant piece of research by John Ashdown Hill of the Richard III Society finding her descendants in the seventeenth generation would not have helped confirm the identity of the remains of Richard III.

William Hobbys, was doctor to the princes, as well as most of the Yorkist Family. Hobbys was the first sergeant surgeon, a role as the monarch's personal surgeon, including caring for him on the battle field. Hobbys was appointed by Edward IV, and as you know my dear colleague from the Middlesex Hospital, Mr. Edward Handley, is your current employee as sergeant surgeon. He is another man with a family history going back to the old Middlesex Hospital.

Hobbys is reputed to have left a diary somewhere,' she continued, 'but it has never been found. Its contents would be absolutely fascinating, and may throw a lot of light on the unanswered questions about the sudden and unexpected death of Edward IV, the diagnosis remains as obscure today as it was then, though he may have had diabetes, and also on the health problems of Edward V. We know Dr Argentine saw Edward V, but we are not sure if Hobbys also saw him and if his jaw problem was a manifestation of some severe underlying disease. Curiously Hobbys did his doctorate at Gonville and Caius College in Cambridge, as did Francis Crick, and for that matter, William Harvey, the discoverer of circulation, and the Australian, Howard Florey, the discoverer of penicillin. Hobbys was one of the most competent doctors in mediaeval England, but unfortunately was divorced in St Pauls when his wife discovered he had been disseminating his DNA around the brothels of Southwark and France. Hobbys was also reputed to have been a regular at the old original Eagle Tavern in Bene't St, Cambridge, where Francis Crick announced to the lunch patrons on February 28th, 1953, that he and James Watson had discovered the structure of DNA! I did my undergraduate degree there.'

'How fascinating,' replied the monarch, 'the traditions of English history go back such a long way, yet are interlinked for generations. I doubt if doctors behave like that these days.'

The Doniach Fellow was aware that she was blushing, but fortunately the monarch was looking at Dr. Crick who appeared somewhat more composed at his colleague's injudicious disclosure. The monarch continued, 'Is it true that Hobbys was an English pioneer of post-mortem examinations?'

'Your Majesty, may I answer' replied Hobbys-Pole, having regained her composure, 'The rumours of time suggest this was so, a document in Cambridge suggests that he taught anatomy and surgical procedures to the undergraduates using the bodies of executed criminals, and that he had also examined many battlefield corpses.'

'Is this procedure still necessary, most non-medical people seem so against it?'

'Your Majesty, may I answer that' interposed Crick, 'If I may say, most doctors in tertiary hospitals perceive a vital need for this, even with the latest electronic T-wave scanners and other tests, some two percent of our patients still die of undiagnosed, yet curable disease. It is our little black box similar to flight recorders; it tells us why the patient and doctor crashed. It can give living members of families' vital information about their risk of hereditary and contagious diseases. We prefer to detect tuberculosis and bowel cancer in the first member of a family, not the second. And of course, it leaves the body looking almost untouched except for the closed midline scar. Apart from a few small samples for analysis, the body contents are restored, and can be done rapidly so funerals are not delayed. Yes we would like to see more being done.'

Crick continued, 'Our laboratory is most interested in DNA testing where there is an unexplained medical or historical mystery, hence the interest in the Princes in the Tower. We would also be fascinated to study the DNA of Margaret of Burgundy, formerly Margaret of York, the sister of Edward IV and Richard III to clarify the York genes. However she was buried in the monastery of the Recollects at Malines in Belgium, and the exact location of her tomb is uncertain. We have applied to Brussels to search in conjunction with our colleagues of the University of London archaeological team, however the legislation there is even more complex and difficult than it was prior to Britain leaving the European Union over fifty years ago, the Brexit as it was known. We would also like to analyse the DNA of John of Gaunt and his descendants over the next few generations, as there appears to be uncertainty about parentage with several of them, however we appreciate we risk your displeasure with that line of research!' The monarch nodded in agreement vigorously.

'As you know our team informed the parliamentary debate a decade ago about the ownership of the remains of past monarchs, in the hope we could clarify some issues about hereditary diseases in the Royal Family, particularly the unexplained origin of Queen Victoria's haemophilia, was it a spontaneous mutation in her genes, or was there another false paternity, and perhaps the false paternity occurrences by DNA testing all previous monarchs, but we lost that vote in the Commons. The traditionalists out-numbered the scientists that time. However, we should not take up more of your precious time, we will seek the remains of the other relevant individuals and report back to you.'

'We will submit our draft press release about our findings to your media office to ensure that you approve of this statement before it is leaked to the press this time! Again I apologise most sincerely for the recent inappropriate and inaccurate quote in the press, and for any distress that may have caused. Thank you for listening to us.'

The two doctors bowed and took their leave, while the monarch made a shrewd guess as to the cause of the blushes.

# OXFORD, SEPTEMBER 26TH 1488

William Hobbys lay, pale and breathless, on his bed, his former wife Alice clasped his hand.

He croaked hoarsely, 'Alice, my children, thank you for coming to Oxford, after the death of Richard III, I felt it was safest to hide myself in the academic ancient cloisters of the university, rather than be a well-known identity in the middle of London where any word of my presence may have offended these new Tudors. I believe my life's page is about to close. I face my death with composure; I have attended many who departed this life in much more distress than I feel. I have lived a long life, I am past my sixtieth birthday, when most people have a lifespan of but thirty years, and been more fortunate than many. I have had the honour of serving the Yorkist noble family for quarter of a century. Both King Edward IV and Richard III were pleased to be honorary members of the Barber-Surgeons Guild at my nomination.'

'I have written an epitaph for my gravestone in my will, here Alice, it is in Latin. It says Hic jacet Willelmus Hobbys quondam medicus et cirurgicus illustrissimi domini Ducis Eboric [ensis] et filiorum suorum Regnum Illustrissimorum Edwardi quarti et Ricardi tercij quorum anime et animabus propicietur deus amen. Alice, I know your Latin is not very good, it means *"Here lies William Hobbys formerly doctor and surgeon of the most illustrious Duke of York and of his sons the most illustrious kings Edward IV and Richard III whose soul and souls God assoil, Amen."*'

'I pray the good Lord will look on my life of dedicated service to others, like my father before me, with favour. The world is a changed place in the last three years and I am not sad to leave it, besides my knees are worn out, I seem to have spent so much of the last two score years or more on them. Money has become so much more important than honour and integrity in Henry Tudor's kingdom of spies, fines and tortures in the Tower. It is no wonder he married Elizabeth of York, a true princess with royal blood, when he is base-born from two bastard lines and needed to bolster his right to the throne. God knows why Margaret Beaufort thinks they are all so important when John of Gaunt was almost certainly not one of the sons of Edward III, and the bastard Beauforts have not one drop of blue blood.'

Alice glanced over her shoulder to ensure that only the immediate family were present. If such treason were heard now, a sojourn in the tower would be the minimum penalty.

William Hobbys paused and attempted to recover his strength and speak some more. Alice sat expressionless and his children sobbed quietly around his bed. 'Even God has cursed the Tudor. The sweating sickness which kills so many, yet has no cure, has followed the Tudor since he arrived at Milford Haven, bringing the accursed disease into this country.' Hobbys dropped his voice to a whisper, 'It is even said there is a curse on the Tudors, perhaps from Elizabeth Wydville, the Dowager Queen. The curse states that Henry Tudor's first born son and first born grandson will both die young without children, following which the throne will revert to a child of York. The Tudor appointed Argentine as physician to the young Prince Arthur, we will see if his theology and limited medical skills will counteract a Wydville curse!

Alice crossed herself and looked around, hoping that his voice was inaudible outside the room while Hobbys gasped for breath, and continued, 'Elizabeth and most of England do not know what happened to the sons of Edward IV, but many suspect the conniving hand of the Tudor and his evil mother as their murderers somehow. There are also rumours that Edward V died, and his younger brother, Richard, is in hiding somewhere, however I am perhaps the only living person who knows what happened to them. I may be the only person who knows why King Edward IV died suddenly, and why Edward abruptly changed his mind about doing battle with the French in 1475.'

'My dearest faithful wife, thank you coming back to me in my final hours, I do not deserve your kindness after my er, er... misdemeanours. I beg you to find my diaries at the bottom of my medicine chest under my equipment, and find somewhere to conceal them until the reign of the base Tudor is over, hopefully within a few years, and the Royal Plantagenet blood sits again in its rightful place. It is rumoured in Yorkist circles, the Margaret of Burgundy is coaching her page boy Perkin, to lead a Yorkist army against the Tudor in a few years when he is old enough, so the true heir, Richard of Shrewsbury, the Duke of York can swop roles at the appropriate moment and take the throne. There are secrets in the diaries, some garnered as professional confidences, but the world needs to know the truth about our late Yorkist sovereigns, in particular about the young Princes, and about the integrity of Richard III.

The world needs to know about the pernicious crimes of Margaret Beaufort. The weaknesses of Edward are well known, but not how they impacted on England's foreign policy. Henry Tudor would burn them, and then attempt to twist the truth and destroy my credibility, so hide them till he is no more, then present them to whoever, whichever of the Yorkist bloodline, ascends the throne, so the country will know about the Beaufort spawn.

There is also a map of Middleham Castle where I have buried something special, a religious icon that belonged to the late Queen Anne. My diaries suitably wrapped and placed in a lead container, could be placed there.' Hobbys fell back against his pillow and closed his eyes. He never spoke another word and passed peacefully into the next life just after midnight.

Alice, whose skills in many areas had been underestimated by Hobbys, decided she would add the date at the bottom of his requested grave stone epitaph: Qui quidam Willelmus obiit vicesimoseptimo die mensis Septembris Anno Domini Millesimo CCCClxxxviij.

'William, you silly man, that means "Which certain William died 27th day of the month of September 1488."' said Alice to his still body, 'you never knew I too had a lover after our divorce, coach drivers seem to have more time in bed than surgeons.'

Alice perused his will. He had appointed two colleagues as his executors. He bequeathed his large silver cup and cover, and five pounds annually to the Barbers Surgeons Masters and Wardens to pay for a communal dinner for both men and women, what sort of women, Alice wondered, and for prayers to be said for him annually, well he would certainly need that for more than one a year. Hobbys wanted a marble gravestone made for his grave in Holy Trinity Priory, Aldgate. Alice hoped he had done enough confessing to be permitted burial there. Priests however; did not seem over concerned with visits to prostitutes. Alice wondered where the profits from his gold trading had gone, he had some good advice over the years from Isaac one of his patients, a gold merchant. Probably spent in Southwark she thought.

Then there was a couple of books, one being "Compendium qui adiscit de arto generali" for his young apprentice John Stavely, and other books and equipment for his other apprentices.

So far not much for me, Alice mused, but there never was much for me was there William.

# LONDON 1425

'So where's your husband?' the midwife enquired. Juliana Hobbys gasped between contractions, 'Doing what John always does, caring for his patients and collecting his fees, they all think he is wonderful. He thought his role in this was the conception part, a minute's pleasure for him and too bad about me, and too bad about his family, we always come second to his patients and his costly fees and importance. At least he left me one of his sponges to suck on for pain, he told me it has been soaked in a mixture of opium, mandrake juice, hemlock and henbane diluted with some water, and that normally he would have charged his patient's three pennies for it but I was lucky to have it for free!' Juliana panted in and out briefly, then continued briefly, 'Anyway this is the last one and that's that!'

'I can see the head; one more big push should do it.' encouraged the midwife. A rush of fluid and baby followed by a baby's bellow announced the arrival of a new child. 'Bloody hell,' cried Juliana. 'A boy at last after three girls, he looks just like his father, probably be another bloody doctor, all smarmy to his patients as long as they pay the bill, and so nice to the women in the hospital as long as they remember the poverty and humility vows, and forget the other chastity one with the doctor. That makes them free and available. Only a doctor's wife knows what he is really like! Anyway, John wanted him called William, so that's what he will be.'

# FETTER LANE HOLBORN LONDON 1447

John Hobbys sat back in his chair, relaxing in front of the log fire after the usual long day's work. The large house in Fetter Lane served as both a family home at the back and on the upper floor, and as a medical centre in the front rooms. Situated just north of the River Thames, it was named after a stream running through to the Thames. Although an old suburb dating back to Anglo-Saxon times, it had increased in popularity recently after Henry V had paved the main road running through Holborn, as it was a busy road, not least for the procession of victims from the Tower being taken to Tyburn Hill for some form of painful public execution. He raised his glass of wine to his son. 'Congratulations William, you make your father very proud, you have been my best student, and have completed your apprenticeship with credit. When we started it only took you a few days to grasp the skill of phlebotomy, whether by cutting the vein, or the use of cupping or leeches, and you were very competent in applying clysters without discomfort in a week or two.'

'Thank you Father, you have been an inspiring teacher, and you have a practice full of fascinating cases and challenging problems.' replied William, raising his own glass. 'London has been an amazing place to learn surgery, so many people, is it sixty thousand living here now, so many living in poverty with rickety bones and bad teeth, so many wealthy men with gout and the stone, so many infections coming in to the country from Europe like leprosy and the plague, so many brothels causing genital infections. The city is a whole text of medicine for students, any surgical apprentice in other cities with a fifth of the people might only see a fifth of the problems we study.'

John nodded in agreement, 'There is one exception to that. Perhaps we should visit Paris, it is said to be five times larger than London, indeed it is the largest city in the world, and so many live lives of debauchery and corruption, a surgeon there would be very busy, and perhaps very rich!'

'William, there are a few changes I need to tell you from the last guild meeting. The Fellowship of Surgeons charter commencing twelve years ago has been replaced by a new combined body with the barbers and physicians. The new conjoined college of Barber-Surgeons and Physicians has some extra rules. If your patient is really sick and requires desperate or deadly remedies, you should consult your colleague in the college within two or three days. You will be expected to attend guild dinners, held on the feast days of the twin saints, Cosmas for medicine, Damian for surgery. It will also be a centre for discourse and learning for us all.'

'All fellows will be still expected to behave appropriately as would be expected by God and the king, and, William, to follow the instructions of the guild masters, who can inspect a surgeon's rooms if there is suspected malpractice.'

'I shall look forward to all those meetings Father, the dinners sound admirable occasions, full of interesting discussions as well as excellent food and wine,' William concurred.

'Also I have some excellent news for you which should really please you,' continued the father, 'my recent employer, Richard, the Duke of York, has asked if you would join his household as barber-surgeon, I think he expects there will be a need for our profession amongst his retainers should the dispute between Richard and the she-wolf of Anjou come to open warfare. I would be interested to examine our poor king, none of Henry VI's doctors have any idea what is causing his melancholia or how to fix it, however she hates with a passion anyone who has been involved with the Duke of York.'

John looked around and lowered his voice. 'William, you know they are doing examinations of human bodies after death in the University of Padua in Italy to study anatomy and diseases, and to find out why people die?' 'Yes father.' replied William.

'Well,' said John, 'poor Will who died this morning with pleurisy has no home, no kith or kin, and will have a pauper's grave. Nobody would know if we opened up his chest and looked inside, then sewed him up and sewed him into a sack, although we treated him well with garlic and fenugreek, steam inhalations and regular bleeding, he just went downhill quickly in spite of our treatment. His body is downstairs in the surgery, it would be interesting to have a look inside at his lungs, we could do that tomorrow before our first patient.'

# FETTER LANE THE NEXT MORNING

**W**ill's lifeless pale emaciated body lay on the slab. Poor Will, in life he had not revealed any family, his parents had died, probably of smallpox when he was young, he had no brother nor sister, wife nor children that he mentioned. No friend visited while he was alive, nor claimed his body in death. John picked up a sharp knife and cut through the skin straight down the middle from his neck down to the pubic bone. 'Watch this William, this is how they open the chest in Padua according to the documents I have had sent from the university.'

Picking up an edge of skin over the breast bone or sternum, he separated the skin from the bone peeling it sideways from the sternum between the midline and the knobbly bits where the ribs joined the breastbone, the costo-chondral junctions, till these joints were all visible. Then picking up his heaviest pair of cutters, he chopped through these joints on both sides, and then the two joints linking the clavicles or collar bones with the sternum till the sternum was separated from the rib cage and could be lifted out. He then pulled the two sides of the chest wall sideways till the inside of the chest was visible, some thin yellow fluid ran out over the chest and onto the floor, a foul smell of decomposing body and pus filled the room.

John set about removing the heart by cutting through the great veins running into the heart from above and below, the superior and inferior vena cava, then the two pulmonary arteries linking the heart with the lungs, then the large aorta which emerges from the big muscular left ventricle, and finally the pulmonary veins, which also link the heart with the lungs. Now he was able to lift out the heart from the chest cavity. John then sliced open the heart muscle to peer inside it, and exclaimed in surprise, 'William, look at this heart, here is no blood in the heart cavity, nor the great vessels, there is supposed to be blood clots in here, do you think it all gone into this congested lung?'

'Strange,' replied William, 'I don't suppose it has anything to do with cupping, we just removed the standard amount, but that is supposed to be a feature of people who bleed to death from severe wounds, very strange.'

John slipped his hand under the left lung, feeling for the left main bronchus, the lungs connection to the trachea, the central windpipe, cut through it with his knife and lifted out the lung. It was a pinky colour with many black spots. It has a soft spongy feel and could be compressed between his fingers, so air bubbled out. 'Will had said he had worked in a coal mine and in a metal foundry, perhaps they had caused the black spots.' said John, thinking aloud. He weighed it on the scales and noted a weight of just under a pound. John turned to the right lung, as he slipped his hand into the chest, a collection of thick yellow and red fluid welled up from the cavity over his hands, and down to the floor, adding to the foul stench filling the room. He dissected out the second lung, finding it partially adherent to the chest cavity, noting it to be hard and heavy, weighing two and a half pounds. When he squeezed it more thick yellow stinking pus seeped out between his fingers.

'Well William, he appears to have had what Hippocrates and Maimonides called pneumonia, you know, of course you know, Hippocrates thought the pus should be drained out through the side of the chest wall, I wonder if we should have tried that or if it would have helped, I think it would have been painful.'

'Better some pain than dead.' replied William.

John replaced the heart and lungs into the chest cavity, placed the sternum in place, pulled back the skin edges to the original position and sewed up the chest. Then the two surgeons pushed the body in a sack, sewed up the top, and sent a runner for their cart to convey the remains of Will to a pauper's grave.

Ten minutes later the room had been cleaned, the floor scrubbed, and the smell partially removed by burning a mixture of dried marjoram, lavender and rosemary, and the days surgery commenced. Father and son continued to ponder on their first post-mortem, no one was aware of the procedure fortunately, no consequence followed, though the priest would have not liked it, and they could have had a lot of trouble in the church court. They also pondered the findings, why was the heart empty, and would they have saved Will's life by draining his chest.

# BAYNARD'S CASTLE LONDON, JANUARY 1447

Hobbys knelt before the Duke of York. Anxiety was written all over his face. This was to be his first independent position as a barbersurgeon without the benefit and safety of his father standing right behind him. His father had been a superb teacher, knowledgeable, compassionate, and decisive, with skilled hands, but was never disdainful or unpleasantly critical of his students, he would listen politely to their answers and dissect them thoughtfully. He treated his son and all his students with similar courtesy and they all blossomed under his tutelage. Now he was not there with his experience and wisdom, Hobbys would have to make his own diagnoses, and treat as he saw fit, and amongst his first patients would be the household of the second mightiest man in the kingdom, many said the mightiest noble who should be the king, but they said such treasonous words quietly.

The Duke sat on a carved bejewelled chair on a dais at the end of the great hall, in the London home of the House of York, wrapped in ermine robes looking for all the world like a king. 'Stand up young Hobbys, your father John tells me you are more skilled than he was when he ended his apprenticeship, I would like you to join my household as he tells me he is no longer up to the rigors of campaigning.

You can be of more value to us than my finest hundred archers. Your father's wisdom enabled my troop to avoid an outbreak of smallpox while campaigning in France. He also treated the wounded soldiers with great skill, enabling them to return to fighting quickly. Somerset and Suffolk, God rot their souls, avoid us in battle at the moment, but are not above slipping a poisoner into my kitchen. Attending childbirth will be another important duty. You will be aware that my mother Anne Mortimer, the great grand-daughter of Lionel of Antwerp, the first Duke of Clarence, and the second son of Edward III, from whom my superior claim to the throne comes, died giving birth to me.'

Richard looked sideways at his wife, Cecily Neville with an affectionate smile, 'My dearest wife, the beautiful Rose of Raby has produced our children so far mostly with courage and success, however, it will be your responsibility Hobbys, with her midwife to ensure we produce many more little Yorkists to strengthen our family and provide this country with better governance. Thus there are many important duties we will need you to perform.'

Hobbys bowed, a little anxious as the vagaries of childbirth may overwhelm the greatest physician's skills.

The Duke continued, 'I fear I am about to be sent to Ireland as some sort of exile, though the traitors around the king say I will be the protector of Ireland. No doubt I will be back to help run this country with strength and safety, when we may well need your skills to repair a few battle scars, hopefully more of that upstart Somerset's men than mine. We expect you will be able to emulate your father surgical skills which saved many of my men lives during the French campaigns. Had the king's incompetent advisers seen fit to finance our campaign and provide adequate soldiers we would be sitting in Paris today.'

'Your Grace,' replied Hobbys, still on one knee, 'My father is too kind, he is a most competent teacher and surgeon, and I think pleased to transfer me from his expense sheet to that of your household!' Hobbys stood up as indicated by a wave of the Duke's hand and continued, 'It will be a great honour to serve your household to the best of my ability wherever your duties take you.'

Richard gestured to a pair of grizzled old warriors beside him, 'Master Hobbys, these two brave gentlemen are Sir William Oldhall, the former speaker of the House of Commons before Suffolk and Somerset grasped power and set about ruining the country, and Sir John Falstof, my chief adviser on French claret amongst other things. They have my complete confidence, you will receive communication from us via these loyal Englishmen, should I require your assistance with problems of a medical nature.'

The next few years passed without overtaxing Hobbys new skills, the horrendous plague which killed a third of the English population was a hundred years in the past, there was an occasional leper to isolate and wounds from the jousting yard and weapons training to suture and bind, though most of this was with blunted lances and swords. Cecily Neville, the Duchess of York produced babies like shelling peas, Hobbys was pleased not to have to perform difficult deliveries with the risk of being responsible for the death of the Duke's heir. Their first daughter Joan and their first son Henry had died shortly after birth long before Hobbys became the Duke's physician, but now they had a daughter Anne, and two sons, Edward and Edmund. Hobbys checked the Duke's children as they grew noisily, rumbustiously and arrogantly encouraged by the Duke's perception of the status of his family.

Young Edward and Edmund often told him of his lowly status, and behaved badly, uncontrollably, such that on occasions he had given them both a well-deserved wallop on their noble bottoms over his knee when unobserved by the Duke or Duchess. They agreed neither boys nor surgeon would inform the Duke of their deplorable behaviour, neither the cause of their chastisement, nor of their punishment, as both surgeon and sons would earn the Duke's wrath. Hobbys took the chance to acquaint himself with more medical classics from his father's library on their trips to Westminster Palace. However, in 1447 the clouds of war were gathering on the horizon.

# FETTER LANE, MARCH 1447

Father and son sat by the fire after another challenging day enjoying a bottle of pinot noir, a new Belgian varietal recently appearing in London. 'Better than some of that watered down French rubbish they have been sending us ever since Agincourt,' opinioned John, when there was a thunderous knock on the door.

Juliana opened the door cautiously to be confronted by a large man, clothed against the continued winter icy blasts, with a very red face, and voice to match his girth. 'Well madam, are you going to admit a very cold messenger from the Duke of York to speak to the surgeons?'

William recognised the voice of Sir John Falstof, and welcomed him into the house. Falstof sat himself in William's seat by the fire, grasped the bottle of red wine and drained the remaining half without taking a breath. 'Jove, that's good, what is it? another bottle may prevent me dying of cold.'

After another liberal goblet, Falstof addressed his curious audience. 'There may be some work for you two soon, you will have heard that, King Henry's uncle, the Duke of Gloucester has just died, some saying poisoned by the devil French queen and her false advisers. My master requests that you should visit his kitchen soon and give advice of poisons to his official food taster.

This means that Richard, Duke of York, our Lord and master, is now next in line to the throne, yet has been excluded from the councils of the nation by lesser jealous nobles. William de la Pole, the Duke of Suffolk is now the most powerful man in the government. The Beauforts, the offspring from the doubly adulterous relationship of John of Gaunt, supposedly the third son of Edward III, and his mistress, Katherine Swynford, although born illegitimate, seek power claiming to be close relatives of the king and to have been legitimised by act of parliament, a dubious law in the eyes of the Duke of York.'

Falstof drained the remains of the second bottle after John and William had ensured some of their new expensive wine went into their own glasses.

'Edmund Beaufort heads that faction, he seeks to be granted the title of the second Duke of Somerset by next year, a Dukedom no less for a bastard line. Somerset and York have now developed a deadly animosity as Somerset now sees himself as the legitimate heir to the throne. Somerset and Suffolk are combining to humiliate York, they replaced him in France as military commander before his term had expired after depriving him of funds and troops to ensure military failure. Suffolk is half the warrior that Duke Humphrey was, he will lose all our possessions in France.' Falstof looked around for a third bottle unsuccessfully.

'These two incompetents wish to send the Duke of York to Ireland, may be next year or the year afterwards with the title of King's Lieutenant in Ireland, we all know this is an undesirable post tantamount to political exile, while all the time the government of the country is slipping into chaos under a weak indecisive king, dominated by the she-devil, his unpopular grasping French wife, Margaret of Anjou, and her favourites.'

'So masters Hobbys,' continued the now warm and increasingly jovial Falstof, 'the Duke of York would like you to visit his kitchen immediately to give your advice on poisons, and to have a bag of surgical equipment at the door, with immediate availability to your horse and wagon to attend any battlefield that may transpire soon,' Falstof paused and looked around,

'Pee-know nawah, did you call it, I don't suppose you have a second bottle we can enjoy?'

York's knights did not return for two years, however Hobbys was kept well informed of events by the merchants of London who all kept their ears to the ground for information that could affect trade. Most informative was Isaac the convert, a goldsmith. Like many of his predecessors as Jewish goldsmiths and traders in London, he was known as the convert, as those who failed to convert to Christianity were thrown out of England. However, he had let slip to Hobbys once on a Friday that he would be observing the Sabbat the following day.

Isaac and Hobbys had an agreement, Hobbys would treat Isaac's gout for free in return for advance notice of changes in the price of gold, a deal that added to both men's wealth.

# FETTER LANE MAY 3ᴿᴰ 1450

Isaac was sitting in Hobbys surgery with a poultice on his toe giving Hobbys the latest news, 'well my dear physician, sharpen your knives and pack your surgeons bag, I think outright war is getting closer, as you know, Suffolk was impeached for misgovernment, he should have been executed as the scapegoat for this incompetent government, but he was only sent into exile. However, news has just reached me, he was murdered yesterday while crossing the channel to go into exile. Apparently a ship called *Nicholas of the Tower* overhauled Suffolk's ship, and he was then subject to a mock trial by its crew and beheaded! Nobody knows who sails the *Nicholas of the Tower*. Somerset is said to be accusing the Duke of York, but really any stalwart Englishman would have been pleased to wield the axe on Suffolk's incompetent body.'

Isaac winced as Hobbys applied another hot poultice, but continued, 'and secondly my friend, you have heard of the unhappiness in the home counties over the loss of France, and the high taxes imposed by this corrupt government, well an outright rebellion in Essex, Kent and Sussex is about to occur, men are assembling and an Irish former sailor, Jack Cade is planning to lead thousands of men in a march on London. They claim to support Henry VI, but are demanding that the king's councillors should be replaced by the Duke of York.'

Isaac dropped his voice to a whisper, 'my friend, war is approaching, now is a good time to buy gold.'

Jack Cade and his followers failed in their demands, and dispersed when they heard Henry was leading an army to crush the rebellion. Cade died of wounds inflicted during the fighting. York summoned his council in Dublin as England lapsed into a leaderless and lawless mess. Hobbys was always expected to attend such major meetings, should his opinion be required on medical issues, and to keep him informed of developments, such that he might ensure that adequate provisions and assistants were available should an armed struggle eventuate with multiple casualties. He suffered an uncomfortable voyage from Tenby to Dublin, worried all the way about the uncontrolled stateless pirates who inhabited the Irish Sea, yet another failure of the government.

Hobbys walked in through the gates of Dublin Castle for the council meeting, reflecting that it had been built in the reign of England's last totally incompetent king, John. Hobbys sat at the far end of the table, as the Duke commencing planning. York said, 'The country is a shambles, we must leave Dublin and return to England in force to persuade the king to get rid of Somerset and institute some competent government before the place degenerates further.' Whereupon his chief advisors and four thousand troops sailed to England and marched to Westminster. Henry dissembled, promising York a role in government initially, but blocking any of York's suggested reforms.

By 1452, York realised that discussion and polite suggestions were getting nowhere. Sir John Falstof arrived in Fetter Lane requesting William to load up his wagon and prepare to expect casualties. Falstof looked around the room optimistically. 'And Master Hobbys, if you have any more of that Belgian red wine, you could bring a couple of bottles, so we call celebrate a Yorkist Victory.' York took up arms, and assembled an army at Blackheath, only to find his force greatly outnumbered by the king's force. His rebellion collapsed, Hobbys returned home to Holborn having had no battle injuries to treat, and the initial offers to York of a role in government evaporated, it was clear that Somerset and Margaret of Anjou working in Henry's name would not accept York in any position of power.

# FETTER LANE AUGUST 25TH 1453

'Hanah' complained Isaac, 'my dear physician, I have a new problem today, an embarrassing one, I paid a visit to Southwark last week to celebrate a special business deal, how foolish, but the kussit, such tzitzi!' Hobbys didn't understand the words, but caught the drift.

'Now my friend I have a dreadful itch, while you examine and treat me let me tell you what is happening in England.'

Hobbys peered at Isaac nether quarters seeing little crab like insects crawling in the hairs and causing a rash partly from bites and partly from scratching. 'Isaac, you have pubic lice, I shall remove as many as possible and apply oil of hyssop. My friend, you should avoid the ladies for a month, and send the one you know to me for a check.'

'Hanah' replied Isaac, 'all of them? Anyway let me tell you, you heard that Cecily Neville, the Duke's wife, has persuaded all her relatives, the powerful and influential Neville family to throw their lot in with York, in part motivated by their rivalry with the Percy family for the control of the North. Although these are two great different families, they are all so closely related, do they fight because they are related, or does such close consanguinity cause some hereditary insanity? You have heard that King Henry appears to have gone insane. The government is now clearly in the hands of Margaret and Somerset, in spite of their increasing unpopularity in the country.

Anyway, back to the Percy's and Neville's. Henry Hotspur Percy, who was killed fifty years ago rebelling against Henry IV, was a violent man. Yet he was the son of a Percy, Henry, the first Earl of Northumberland, and of a Neville, Margaret the daughter of Ralph, the second Lord Neville of Raby. Joan Beaufort and Ralph Neville, the first earl of Westmoreland, married their daughters to the Dukes of York, Norfolk and Buckingham, while another married Henry Percy, the second Earl of Northumberland. They are all so interrelated, why can't they share their huge wealthy estates?'

Isaac paused to survey Hobbys ministrations, wondering what were the lasses' names, and continued, 'anyway, the big news of today is that the Percy's and the Neville's fought a battle yesterday.' Hobbys marvelled as always at Isaac's information, he must have a network of informants all over the country with very efficient post-riders.

Isaac continued, 'it was an inconclusive battle fought between the two families at Heworth Moor on August 24th 1453. Thomas Percy, the Lord of Egremont, attacked a Neville wedding party, the Neville's rallied round Richard, the Earl of Salisbury and broke through the Percy forces making good their escape with few casualties on either side, but both sides now seek open revenge. What a cowardly thing to do, attacking a wedding party, even if you don't like the dynastic connections it makes. Poor Thomas Neville, the earl's second son, not only has a threatening mother in law, but a threatening war party of Percy's'

Isaac dropped his voice, 'My sources in Westminster Palace tell me that Margaret of Anjou after eight years of childless marriage to the king, is expecting a child in about six weeks. I'm told that Henry knows little of this, but will be as surprised as the York's and the people of England. My source tells me that Somerset has been visiting the queen's apartments at night for private audiences. He may have had more personal input into the pregnancy than will be admitted in Westminster!'

Following the birth of Edward, of Lancaster, the new Prince of Wales, the York and Lancastrian factions surveyed each other with mistrust watching for advantage. The increasing power and popularity of the combined York and Neville faction could not be denied during the king's period of insanity, Richard became protector of the Realm, and his brother-in-law, Richard Neville, the Fifth Earl of Salisbury became Chancellor, while Somerset was detained in the Tower. Hobbys was disappointed not to be asked to see the old king, to see if his diagnostic and therapeutic skills could solve the problem, not that the Yorkists' would wish him to help old Henry recover. The revolving doors of power changed again in December 1454, when Henry regained his wits, and Somerset was released from the Tower to resume control with Margaret. Open warfare appeared inevitable, and Hobbys was summoned to attend the Duke with his wagon of supplies and some apprentices. Both sides assembled armies and met one more time north of London for final negotiations, but neither side had any intention of conceding ground on any issue, and many eagerly anticipated testing their cause before God on a field of battle. Armed conflict inevitably broke out soon after.

# ST ALBANS 22ND MAY 1455

The smaller Lancastrian army took up defensive positions in town which were attacked by York's men when negotiations failed. Initially York's men made little progress and suffered many casualties which if still showing signs of life, were carried to Hobbys wagon. The Earl of Warwick led a surprise flanking movement destroying the Lancastrian defences. The York faction were successful, and the king was captured. Somerset and two other leading Lancastrians, Henry Percy, the Earl of Northumberland, the head of the Percy faction, and Lord Clifford were all killed. There were some hundred killed Lancastrian soldiers, and a lesser number of York's men died, perhaps sixty.

One of the unfortunate soldiers taken to Hobbys' cart had an arrow deeply embedded in his arm just above the elbow. Hobbys offered a piece of linen soaked in opium and henbane for the unfortunate man to suck. The barbed arrow head was too deep to pull out without severe damage to muscles, vessels and nerves, and Hobbys could feel the hard arrow tip just below the skin on the other side of the arm. Hobbys trimmed off the shaft of the arrow leaving some three inches remaining, then requested his assistants to hold the man and his arm such that he could not move. He tapped the end of the arrow sharply with his mallet. The unfortunate soldier gave a yelp of pain as blood gushed from his arm, and the arrow head popped out with little damage beyond a skin tear. His struggles were unavailing as the assistants held him firmly. Hobbys grabbed the arrow head pulling it quickly through the skin, then clamped a swab over the wound, as a smile spread over the soldier's face. 'Oh that feels better, thanks master Hobbys.'

He jumped off as another was laid on the cart. He had a leg severed through the thigh and had apparently rapidly bled to death before Hobbys could ligate the large femoral artery. Although the body was warm, he showed no sign of life. Hobbys placed a bowel of water on his chest which appeared not to move, nor were there any ripples of water as occurred when the chest was moving. He could not hear any breathing or sounds from the heart when he applied his ear to the chest, and the man did not respond when shaken. Hobbys looked around, nobody was looking, they all were cheering as victory was declared. Hobbys opened up his chest, as his father had shown him, on his wagon, where no one could see he was working on a corpse. Most of the victorious army had now found one of the many alehouses in town. As expected he found the chambers of the heart and the major vessels depleted of blood. This was what the texts from Padua described, though they did not explain why careful therapeutic cupping yielded the same finding. Hobbys sewed the chest back up such that the man looked as though he had a major chest wound which had been repaired.

After the battle the Duke of York again became the protector with most of the power, and Hobbys returned to his home and practice in London.

# FETTER LANE, HOLBORN, LONDON 1455

John and William Hobbys sat collapsed by the fireplace each with a large goblet of claret in their hand. The Bells of Temple Church could be heard distantly ringing midnight.

'That was a very long day's work.' said John. 'William my son, it is time we discussed your future. One day surgeons may be recognised for their skills and paid more, but at this time, physicians are more esteemed for their knowledge of medicine and theology.' They sipped thoughtfully, wearily on their wine.

John continued, 'when we established the Fellowship of Barber Surgeons twenty years ago, with all its rules, it was seen by the conjoined College of Physicians and Surgeons with only twelve years' seniority, as being the place for blood and brawn, not suitable for clever doctors. Mind you the conjoined college really only lasted in any effective form for a couple of years, and by the time you were born it had lost leadership and influence. You have become a skilled surgeon, that last leg amputation took you only a few minutes. That man already had gangrene of his foot and surely would have died without your operation. You have followed the regulation of twenty years ago to 'well and truly behave in the saving of God's and the King's people and to abide by the decisions of the Guild Masters, and to respect the right of your fellow members to practice. The masters have never had to exert their right to inspect our premises for suspected malpractice.'

John drained his glass and resumed, 'it is time to improve your qualifications. With the financial support and encouragement of the Duke of York, I have set aside sufficient funds for you to attend Balliol College at Oxford University for three years. With your knowledge of the classic texts of medicine and surgical anatomy, you should be able to achieve a bachelor's degree in half the time of others. Unfortunately, many of the students attending Oxford pass their time in ale houses and bawdy houses, but I think you are more mature than that. You should start with the Hilary term next month.'

William raised his goblet to his father, then drained his wine. 'Father you have always been most helpful with my practice of surgery, I appreciate the chance to improve my skills and will look forward to the tuition of the greatest medical teachers in the land.'

John surveyed his son silently, and after collecting his thoughts, raised another topic, 'My son, it is time you were a respectable married man, it will enhance your status in the eyes of the guild and your patients, and provide your parents with the pleasure of grandchildren. Alice is a most delightful young lady, your mother and I wonder what is delaying your proposal of marriage to her.' Hobbys thought briefly, wondering if he could ever confine his attention to only one lady, having developed an increasing addiction in his limited time off for the stews of Southwark. He could see the benefits for his career and responded, 'Father, you are right there, she is a most virtuous lady who I am sure will make me very happy, I will consider your suggestion most carefully.'

# AUTUMN 1455

Alice's pale thighs gleamed in the candle light, the one candle she had reluctantly accepted should remain lit. Her nightdress had been pulled up well above her knees, superficially it was enticing, but represented the most she was prepared to expose willingly. Her face showed extreme discomfort and embarrassment, she knew the horrendously painful and embarrassing moment about which her mother had warned her was imminent.

'I suppose this will not be your first time William?' she enquired.

Hobbys reflected that their relationship had been good so far. Alice's father had been delighted to accept William's request for his hand in marriage, William seemed a rising star as a surgeon, a surgeon in the employ of the House of York, in London, with an increasingly lucrative practice. Alice had seemed delighted with their courtship, though very shy and reluctant to engage in any physical contact beyond permitting a chaste kiss on the cheeks.

The wedding in the Temple Church of Holborn included the old pagan tradition of hand fasting with ribbons. Hobbys felt he was a bit of a pagan at heart and did not complain. The ceremony had progressed uneventfully and rapidly thanks to the priest's known enjoyment of a few classes of wine when asked to the subsequent wedding reception, in fact John Hobbys, the priest and his new father-in-law had an uproarious time. Hobbys had suffered some dubious stories told by his surgical colleagues, and enjoyed some of his father's best wines, and ultimately he was finally alone with Alice in the best room of 'Ye Olde Cheshire Cheese' a tavern near the Fleet River that had once been a Carmelite monastery. Hobbys reflected that Alice was therefore unlikely to be the first young lady to lose her virginity here as this was suspected to have been the Abbott's room. He evaded the question as tactfully as possible.

'My dearest Alice, I shall do my best to cherish you carefully such that you experience little discomfort, and perhaps even some pleasure, as I most certainly will be the first man to know you intimately.'

Hobbys subsequent pleasure was such that he felt he might manage to honour his vow of fidelity, at least, for a while. Alice appeared pleased that the ordeal was over, that it had not been as bad as her mother had warned, and happy that Hobbys had really enjoyed being with her.

# JANUARY 1456

Immediately after his honeymoon, Hobbys entered the Court of Balliol College, Oxford, to be welcomed by the college beadle, Robbie and directed initially to his accommodation, followed by a tour of the College with all the new students. Some time was spent in the library reviewing the outstanding collection of ancient tomes, including *De Proprietatibus Rerum* by Bartholomew Glanville and *Compendium Medicinae* by Gilbertus Anglicus. Robbie looked at Hobbys thoughtfully, 'It's good to have some more mature students amongst the young hot heads, at least you won't be spending all your time in the brothels and taverns.' For the next three years Hobbys immersed himself in all facets of university life, in which academic study featured little initially much to Robbie's disapproval, but progressively more as final exams loomed closer in the final year.

News of external events reached them on an irregular basis. Over the next few years after the Battle of St. Albans, Margaret and her young Prince Edward sought to recover influence. York was outmanoeuvred as he could not take arms directly against the king since this would be treason, he could only seek to remove the Lancastrians from influence. This all seemed of limited relevance compared with the pleasures of student life.

# FETTER LANE 1458

John shook his son warmly by the hand, 'Warden of the Guild of Barber-Surgeons, that's an eminent position and a credit to your abilities. Congratulations! However, by next year, you will have graduated as a physician. You will be too academic for a mere bunch of manual artisans!'

'Thank you father, I hear that the Duke of York has appointed two of his son's Edward of March and young Richard as patrons of the guild. It is appropriate that our skills should be recognised at the highest level. Well, I must be returning to Oxford now.'

# OXFORD JANUARY 1459

Hobbys stood in the quadrangle of Balliol College sharing handshakes, some ale and a few last ribald jests with his fellow graduates. He took a last look around at the old hall, the library where he had done some studying to catch up in his final year, where there were some fascinating books donated by John Gray, now the Bishop of Ely, but a former student at Balliol and former University Chancellor, and lastly he gazed at the Master's Chamber, to which he and his fellow undergraduates had been summoned more than once for some misdemeanours in the town.

The Master thought Hobbys should enter the priesthood as well as medicine, but the nearest he had come to the religious life as a student was regular attendance at the establishment founded by a former Bishop of Hereford, John Trellick, known as Trellick's Inn, now student quarters and used for various more pagan practices than imagined by the Bishop. After many attempts, Hobbys had finally mastered the secrets of the fuddling cup, an assembly of three interconnected vessels which had to be drunk in the right order to prevent one from spilling good drink over one's clothing. It was certainly best attempted as the first drink of the night rather than the last when it would usually go to waste to the amusement of his fellow students of debauchery.

Hobbes father had loaned him money for his studies, unaware that most of it had been spent there on ale, and young ladies. His vow of fidelity had sadly only lasted a little over a year. Initially reluctant, he accepted his fellow students' viewpoint that the ladies of easy virtue in town were an essential part of undergraduate education. Hobbys also reflected that he still owed his father ten pounds or more, and unfortunately the time for some work to repay his generosity was rapidly approaching.

'So its farewell Master William, or I should say Dr 'obbys now you can lecture on the aphorisms of Hippocrates. I hear you can get twenty shillings a lecture. Even more eminent than your position last year as warden of the guild of barber-surgeons." Said Robbie, the college beadle. "Oxford will be a lot quieter without you lot, you've been rowdy even for medical students. I don't suppose you will even think of poor Sarah anymore, let alone provide for her.'

'Well, Robbie, thanks for looking after us, I won't be called doctor till I finish my doctorate in medicine at Cambridge in another three years.' said Hobbys in surprise. 'I thought we studied hard and mostly behaved well, and as for Sarah, her husband shouldn't have spent so long away tending the squire's fields in Leicestershire. Anyway Sarah is happy to be having a baby, and it might have been fathered by any of us, not just me.'

Hobbys was briefly lost in thought, Sarah had been a voluptuous serving wench in Trellick's Inn, had he not been in the company of other drunken students, he might not have succumbed to her very willing and available charms. Unfortunately, having had his conscience dulled by alcohol the first time he committed adultery, it did not seem to trouble him half as much the next time, or the times after that.

Robbie interrupted his reveries. 'Well doctor, you were a dark horse, last in theology was expected, John Wycliffe would have been unimpressed, did you know he was here in Balliol a hundred years ago, I guess you didn't see his bible in the library. But first in Latin, French, Greek, Arabic, anatomy and dissection, and second in botany with the University gold medal, now that was a surprise package. And you did it in only three years, most of your friends here took six to eight years, though they spent most of their time with ale and wenches. I expect your previous years as a surgeon helped with anatomy.' said the beadle.

'Thanks Robbie, all my father's texts helped with the languages, I had been reading them for over ten years,' laughed Hobbys. 'I hope to put that to good use, perhaps you may hear of me again. I have been surgeon to the Duke of York, the next step up would be the King's personal surgeon. Don't forget royalty has been here, after all Humphrey, the late Duke of Gloucester, was also here, and they may think highly of Balliol College!'

'That's as likely as me becoming the College Master!' responded the beadle. 'However you might find your fencing skills useful should you get in with that warring lot. I remember you black and blue all over with bruises after the match with Cambridge University, but you did win – is that why they call it a blue?'

Hobbys laughed, 'My opponent from Cambridge was useless with the rapier, and tried to turn it into a wrestling match until the umpire imposed fencing rules! Farewell Robbie.' and then he called to the coachman, 'Off we go.' and the horse set off with a clatter on the cobbles, taking Hobbys into an unknown future and the next stage of his life.

The fortunes of war swung again with minor encounters till York was confronted with a larger force at Ludford, and fled, York and Edmund to Ireland, Salisbury, his son, Richard Neville, the Earl of Warwick, and York's eldest son, Edward, the Earl of March fled to Calais. York's younger two sons, George and Richard were left to the mercy of the Lancastrians in Ludlow Castle. Hobbys, never far from York's side was always on the move and busy with injuries from the various skirmishes.

# FETTER LANE JULY 10, 1460

Isaac sat before Hobbys, his skin and eyes a pale yellow, his abdomen grossly swollen, 'my friend, Master Hobbys, what is becoming of my health, I have felt unwell since adding the wine trade to my family's trading in gold, which you know we have done for a thousand years or more. You know the French hate us Jews, even those of us now converted to your Christianity, do you think they have tried to poison me? Are my Fathers angry with me for neglecting the family business, what do you think my friend?'

Hobbys put Isaac up on his couch, noting the red palms, the spidery blood vessels on his nose and chest, and the yellow colour of his eyes. Hobbys palpated Isaac's abdomen and tapped it noting a transmitted thrill from the fluid inside.

'My dear Isaac,' responded Hobbys, 'the French have indeed poisoned you, though you have acquiesced in the process, how many bottles of their fluid do you drink a day?'

'Ah, my dear friend it is hard to say, my business friends and I share a glass of two during our discussions, it seems to help our bargaining, maybe four or five bottles a day with my various partners and business associates during several meetings, is it bad for me? it seems good for business.'

Hobbys said gravely, 'You have liver cirrhosis, from the alcohol, let your business associates have all the wine, while you have none on your physician's orders for a year. It will help your liver and your profit. So what news do you have today? you always know something we have not yet heard in London.'

Isaac looked around furtively, and in a conspiratorial whisper said, 'You knew the Earls of Warwick, Salisbury and March had re-entered the country after the fiasco at Ludford, well yesterday their forces battled those of the French Queen at Northampton. After more useless negotiations, Warwick attacked. Lord Grey of Ruthin changed sides to the Yorkists on the battlefield, providing they would support him in his dispute with Lord Fanhope. After that betrayal, the fighting lasted less than an hour with the route of the remaining Lancastrians. The Duke of Buckingham, the Earl of Shrewsbury, Lord Egremont and Lord Beaumont were killed trying in vain to protect old King Henry. Henry was captured and is now a hostage of Warwick. Your master, the Duke of York is reputed to be returning to England to claim the throne. My friend, load up your medical wagon, and I have a special price for gold just for you today.'

Richard did indeed cross from Ireland now with the intention of claiming the throne. He became protector and heir to the throne, but again had not allowed for the determination of Margaret of Anjou and her forces. Richard retired to his castle in Sandal where Hobbys re-joined his service.

# CAMBRIDGE 1460

**H**obbys wondered which would be the optimum college for his doctorate; Clare was founded by the old Duke of Lancaster, Queen's by the she-wolf, and King's by Henry, the mad king. None of them seemed appropriate for a doctor employed and subsidised by the Duke of York. Clare College also had a rule that students must report all other students seen visiting taverns too often or houses of ill-repute, a strange concept that would have had most students in Oxford on report! Magdalene was for student monks, not a college likely to accept him. Clearly the best choice was Gonville Hall which had a reputation for medical degrees.

Hobbys entered Gonville court in Cambridge, admiring the beautiful stone buildings constructed from stones taken from the old Ramsay Abbey, including the seventy-year-old chapel at the centre, the old hall containing the library, and the master's lodge, a place he hoped to attend a little less often than its counterpart in Balliol, to commence study for his doctoral thesis. His fellow doctoral students appeared significantly older and more serious than those he had recently farewelled in Oxford. The college beadle, Wilfred, showed the new students around, commencing with the library and ending with their accommodation. "So Master Hobbys, doing medicine are we? You must meet Master John Argentine, one of the cleverest students this university has ever seen, he's at King's in his final year of his medical degree, before going on to a master's degree, you could learn from 'im. He knows more theology than the dean, and knows everything about astronomy. He writes poetry and is the best chess player in the university, he could certainly teach you a thing or two.' announced the beadle.

'So can he amputate a leg or diagnose gut shot, or even use a sword.' Seethed Hobbys, 'You are probably unaware that I have already graduated in medicine from Oxford and I am here to complete a doctorate, Mr Argentine may be interested to hear of my many years' experience.' He discussed his proposed studies with the master of the college. When he first raised the topic of post-mortem examinations, he met with the full disapproval of the Catholic Church in the person of the master, a doctor of theology, and dean of the cathedral.

Hobbys said, 'Let me explain my reasons. Removal of internal organs was first performed over 4000 years ago by the ancient Egyptians in a religious ceremony to enable them to preserve bodies, a process we now call mummification. They believed that outward disfigurement of a dead body might prevent passage into the afterlife, so they removed the internal organs through very small incisions with great skill. In this famous seat of learning we acknowledge the ancients Greeks as the forefathers of scholarly learning. As an undergraduate at Oxford, we were instructed in grammar, logic, rhetoric, mathematics, geometry and astronomy, we read the classical texts by Hippocrates and Galen, and more recent books such as Antidotarium by Nicholas of Salerno and De Febribus by Judaeus.'

Hobbys was hoping he had remembered some of the rhetoric, while the master listened attentively and nodded.

'The Greeks were the first nation to really revere knowledge and learning, arts and music, and to study the human body. The ancient Greeks term for a post-mortem was autopsia, derived as you would know as a Greek scholar yourself, from autos meaning self, and opsis meaning eye, translated as to see for oneself. In ancient Greece, Aristotle recommended animal dissection, Herophilus of Chalcedon who lived from 335-280BC performed public dissections of human cadavers, discovering the prostate gland and duodenum. He may have performed vivisection on public criminals.

Hobbys paused, 'That may be deserved sometimes, but I do not propose that.'

He continued, 'Galen, one of the great figures of classical medicine and anatomy performed public examinations of live animals, and may have performed post-mortem examinations of cadavers, he is certainly known to have examined some skeletons. Erasistratus, who lived from 304-250 BC, is another well-known Greek. He was an anatomist and physician to the King of Syria. He described the anatomy of the brain and was the first to believe that the heart was a pump, all detailed knowledge learned from post-mortems. Our knowledge of anatomy was first developed by these ancient scholars; without which we would be less able to practice healing today.

One hundred and fifty years before the birth of our lord, the Romans had developed clear circumstance when such examinations were permitted as part of their legal system. Julius Caesar, arguably the greatest Roman of them all, who first brought civilisation to England had a post-mortem establishing that he had been stabbed twenty-three times by other Roman senators, but that the second wound would was the fatal one. Even after death, he was able to assist in the development of medicine. But for the civilisation of Rome, Christianity may not have come to England, perhaps till much later, and we would not be sitting in this great Christian centre of learning. As you know, the centres of learning in the dark ages passed into the hands of the Arabic people. The scholars amongst them, though Muslims, were men of enlightened tolerance, able to discuss religious differences with intelligence and harmony.

Anenzoar and Ibn al-Nafis were pioneers of medical knowledge in their time. Anenzoar, or Ibn Zuhr as known by the Arabs, was born in Seville, Andalusia, in 1094, so he was partially exposed to Christianity.

He was a Muslim physician and surgeon, recognised as the best of his era, a contemporary of two other great medical leaders of the time, Averroes and Maimonides. He performed post-mortem examinations and wrote a book, the Book of Simplification Concerning Therapeutics and Diet, which has since been translated into Latin. His knowledge of anatomy, partially acquired through dissection advanced surgical expertise. He even managed to place a tube in the wind pipe, or trachea of a goat, a technique that could save the life of patients with a blocked upper airway.

Pope Alexander V was born in Crete in about 1339 as Peter Phillarges. He tried to unite the Church in spite of the schism of Popes, and ultimately became Pope himself in 1409, but within ten months he died suddenly. His successor, Pope John XXIII was suspected of poisoning him to become pope himself. He had a post mortem examination performed by Pietro D'Argelaia who thought he found traces of poison. Post-mortem examination has been performed for some two thousand years by the great intellectual forefathers of medicine and philosophy to advance knowledge, on eminent people including a Pope. It provides the great people of the nation with protection from malefactors who may be detected through evidence provided by post mortem examination.'

The master continued to listen intently without interruption, making a few notes. Hobbys felt he was making a good impression and continued.

'My interest is in battlefield wounds, why does blood loss cause death, why are head wounds fatal without much blood loss, does bleeding help injuries. In a small way I hope my studies, my proposed doctorate and future research will reflect credit on these august halls of learning and will help to advance medical knowledge, for sadly we live in a time of war in what is normally a green and pleasant land.'

'Guy de Chauliac, a French Physician of last century, the author of a seminal surgical text, the Chirugia Magna wrote "A surgeon who does not know his anatomy is like a blind man carving a log". My studies will enhance my knowledge of anatomy. Finally, I would like to offer you my services as a doctor both with a university qualification and with the experience of more than a decade as a surgeon, to teach anatomy and surgical operations to the university students of your college. It will revise my skills, and enable them to learn first on a patient who can feel no pain.'

However; once Hobbys had explained his interest, the history of such examinations, and the value of student teaching, the Master agreed reluctantly suggesting a covering title such as wound and trauma evaluation and management.

The master further enlightened Hobbys in the traditions of the College, as a doctoral candidate, and with the Duke of York as his sponsor, he would be considered as one of the fellows, and therefore permitted to walk on the grass, and obliged to attend the second sitting of dinner, known as Formal Hall. He would enter gowned when the gong was rung and the students would all stand. Hobbys as a God fearing doctor would be expected to read the College Latin grace, 'Benedic, Domine, nobis et donis tuis quae ex largitate tua sumus sumpturi; et concede ut, ab iis salubriter enutriti, tibi debitum obsequium praestare valeamus, per Jesum Christum dominum nostrum; mensae caelestis nos participes facias, Rex aeternae gloriae.'

Hobbys thought to himself that he had done well to transfer to Cambridge for his doctorate, rather than remain in Oxford where his reputation was not entirely that of a God-fearing scholar.

# SANDAL MAGNA CASTLE, 29TH DECEMBER 1460

Hobbys sank to his knees; he could not recall any offence that he had committed that could cause him to be summoned again into the presence of the greatest magnate in England. His previous work for the Duke seemed satisfactory and well received. He wondered if young Edward, now the Earl of March had complained to his father about Hobbys giving him a few spankings when Edward was a boy. He had been arrogant when a small boy, claiming that he would become much more important than a mere barber, and that he would wield a real man's sword when he was grown, not just a scalpel which was smaller than a lady's knife!

From what Hobbys had heard he was now a giant of a youth well capable of wielding a double-handed broadsword. Hobbys had worked hard with his patients and further studies since leaving Oxford. He hoped word of his activities outside the lectures and anatomy room had not reached the Duke. There were no blemishes on his professional record or personal life as a qualified doctor. He awaited the arrival and pronouncement of Richard, Duke of York with trepidation.

The Duke of York and his wife, Cecily Neville entered surrounded by a retinue which would befit a king, indeed Hobbys had heard Richard more than ever believed he was entitled by his heritage and divine right to sit on the throne of England. Certainly anyone would be ill-advised to suggest otherwise in such company.

'Ah Master William Hobbys, thank you for coming to see us again. How is your father, John? as you know I know him well, a fine surgeon, the best repairer of battle damaged warriors in all England.'

'Your Grace is too kind, my father was an inspiration to my studies, I learnt a lot at his practice at Fetter Lane in London, he helped me become a member of the guild of barber-surgeons in London, and he has a wonderful library of medical books. But now sadly his health is slowly failing. I fear he may not be with us in a year's time.' Hobbys procrastinated still wondering why he had been summoned. 'How may I render any humble assistance to your Lordship' replied Hobbys, still on his knees.

'Stand up man, we are all equal in our great country. I understand that you have studied medicine in Oxford for three years and now have obtained a degree of Bachelor of Medicine.'

'Yes my Lord,' responded Hobbys, rising to face Richard. 'The Lord has looked favourably on my humble efforts, and I was inspired by my father's achievement. He encouraged me to study as a physician for my bachelor's degree at Oxford, and then to seek a doctorate.'

'So, Master Hobbys, I understand that you are now attending Cambridge University to obtain that doctorate in medicine, and that you have refused to enter the priesthood,' continued Richard.

Hobbys, believing he could now see the cause of Richard's complaint, sank back to his knees and replied, 'Your Grace, I am trying to become the best doctor that I can be, I humbly believe that I lack the virtues to become a servant of God, I believe my limited skills are best applied in medicine, but if it pleases your grace, I will endeavour to qualify for the priesthood in spite of my lack of understanding of the ways of our Lord.'

'You idiot Hobbys, I am surrounded by useless priests already, I wish to know if you will continue to work for me now as my personal physician and surgeon with your dual qualifications and training.' asked Richard

'I encourage you to achieve your higher qualification, I encourage you to use the lancet, now fortunately forbidden to my worthless ministers, I need you skills to repair my warriors, especially this week as we face Henry's treacherous and false advisors on the morrow. Some rumours reaching me suggest that the priesthood would not be the optimum choice for you.'

Hobbys wondered what this comment meant, surely he had been moderately discrete at Oxford. 'My Lord, nothing would give me greater pleasure than to be physician to your illustrious household and to your royal personage, I will do my best with my poor skills to measure up to this most honourable position, and to be a worthy successor to my father, should my skills be needed on a battlefield.'

It crossed Hobbys mind that he had been attending an Oxford college founded by a noble, John Balliol, whose son tried but essentially failed to become the king of his country, when his power and then his title were stripped from him by two much more ruthless men, Edward Longshanks and Robert Bruce. He hoped that cycle was not about to repeat around him.

'However may I say, as the physician now responsible for your health and welfare that it is widely reported outside the castle, that the she-wolf of Anjou has thousands of men concealed in the woods, that her honeyed tongue and lascivious body has seduced John Neville back into the Lancastrian fold, and that your greatly outnumbered forces could suffer a terrible defeat on the morrow.' Hobbys continued, 'may I suggest that you should remain within these walls to protect yourself and especially your son Edmund, until your son and heir, Edward, Earl of March arrives with reinforcements. Edmund has scarcely achieved manhood yet, and the she-wolf would seek to slay him.'

'Hobbys, you exceed the position I offer you, never do that again if you wish to remain in my service, I do not need your opinion on military matters, prepare your equipment and assistants for a few wounded on the morrow, hopefully mainly the soldiers of the she-wolf. Edmund is a man and must win his spurs.' roared Richard.

Cecily Neville had maintained a discreet silence to this point, but could not resist adding,

'My dearest husband, you are a mighty warrior, but Master Hobbys may be right, the rumours around the castle say you are outnumbered, why not wait till our dearest son Edward arrives with reinforcements, and then destroy the witch from Anjou.'

'Bah,' said the Duke, 'do you think I need the support of a callow youth, albeit my giant of a son, to win a battle for me? enough nonsense, to bed with all of us, for the morrow will be busy.'

# SANDAL CASTLE DECEMBER 30TH 1460

Richard, Duke of York stood beside his horse, stirrup cup in hand, three leopards on his tunic, and a huge sword beside him. 'Well young Rutland, we are off to reconnoitre the enemy disposition, and once the rest of our troops return from foraging, we shall smash them on the field of battle'

Cecily Neville stood, her thick cape unable to hide her fragile beauty, watching anxiously, her second son was not yet a full grown man, but her husband's blood lust prevented him seeing this. 'My dearest Lord, take care, may God return you safely to us, your force of five hundred men is much smaller than the she-wolf's. Bring my son home unharmed till he is full grown.'

Hobbys standing beside her spoke to the Duke, 'Your Grace, again I seek your permission to come with you to provide both my sword and scalpel as needed, I won trophies for my skills with the rapier while a student at Oxford.'

Richard dismissed the suggestion with a laugh, 'A rapier! a woman's weapon, tell me when you can use a broadsword.' He called to the troop, 'Mount up.' and 'Forward.' They rode out through the portcullis and over the drawbridge for an encounter with destiny.

# SANDAL CASTLE, LATER THE SAME DAY

'**R**iders approaching,' the lookout in the battlements called. 'Call my Lady, the duchess and the doctor,' called the troop sergeant.

The drawbridge was lowered and the portcullis to permit the arrival of a dozen mounted men in Yorkist livery, dirty, blood-stained, exhausted, some bearing severe visible wounds just managing to remain mounted. One climbed off his horse, falling to his knees as Cecily Neville approached. 'Out with it man, where are the duke and my son, what has happened?'

'My lady,' he gasped, 'the worst news possible, oh my God, give me water,' he drank voraciously and started again. 'My Lady, we had gone but five miles to the edge of the forest when we were attacked, cavalry came out of the trees, and infantry men and archers rose from the ground on the other side. After a few volleys of arrows which killed or wounded half our force, their cavalry at least a thousand of them smashed into our side and destroyed what was left of our battle line. I saw the Duke and Thomas Neville go down under the first charge, they died courageously sword in hand fighting bravely against hopeless odds. I was injured and lay on the battlefield, the Lancastrians thought I was dead, but I was able to crawl away later unnoticed.'

'My son, what happened to my son?' cried Cecily

'Oh my Lady, your son and the Earl of Salisbury were captured as they tried to escape, and that foul fiend Clifford beheaded them both there and then. The Duke's body was propped up on an anthill, given a garland of reeds and mocked by Somerset. He went on one knee and said "Hail King, without rule. Hail King, without ancestry. Hail leader and prince, with almost no subjects or possessions." The she-wolf arrived and commanded that all their heads should be impaled on the gates of York with a mock paper crown on the Duke's head.' With that both Cecily Neville and the soldier collapsed to the ground, the Duchess having swooned, and the soldier unconscious from blood loss and wounds.

Hobbys rushed forward cradling the Duchesses head and giving some smelling salts while his assistants conveyed the severely injured men to his treatment room in the castle wall. As the duchess regained her composure and was supported back to her quarters by her ladies in waiting, Hobbys followed to his room to prepare dressings, splints, sutures and medicines for the wounded.

He remained in Sandal Castle expecting capture and worse at any stage till amazing good news filtered through. First, Edward met Jasper Tudor's army at Mortimer's Cross on 2nd February, and after seeing three suns in the sky, a portent of victory, he defeated the Lancastrians. Owen Tudor was captured and beheaded with his head being set on a cross in Hereford Square. Edward returned to London where he was crowned in splendour, though he knew he still had a battle to come shortly.

# CAMBRIDGE UNIVERSITY, MARCH 7ᵀᴴ

The cold winter continued unabated in England, there was no sign of spring. Hobbys was back in Cambridge demonstrating anatomy to an undergraduate class. Three felons had been hung the previous day for the robbery and murder of a town merchant, it was an excellent event for Hobbys, who was always on the lookout for bodies to dissect. A man burst in wearing a parhelion, the three suns on his tabard. 'Excuse me, gen'lemen, I am looking for Master Hobbys, the surgeon to the late Richard, Duke of York, would that be you sir?' He asked looking at Hobbys, the only one present wearing an academic gown.

'Yes sir,' replied Hobbys, 'are you aware you are interrupting a class of great theoretical importance?'

'Sir,' the man replied, 'I come from my master, the great warrior, Edward, Earl of March, proclaimed King of England three days ago. He requests that you, as a surgeon to the House of York, should accompany his army north, where I am sure he will be able to provide you with more bodies than you have....' The man lost his voice when he actually became aware of what was happening before his eyes, he rushed outside and could be heard vomiting. He returned shortly, looking studiously at the floor, and continued, 'will that be alright sir?'

Hobbys explained to the master of the college that he had had a royal summons to accompany the Yorkist army northwards, and almost certainly he would be able to undertake some very helpful practical field work to aid his studies. Then he packed a bag of surgical instruments, donned his thickest clothing and cape, and mounted to follow his messenger west to Royston, the assembly point north of London, on the main road, the old Roman Ermine Street, to the north.

A huge army was camped here, troops arrived from all four corners of the compass to swell the ranks. Hobbys was directed to a tent to the south of the assembly, where a cart drawn by a large carthorse, and bearing two surgical assistants awaited his arrival. Hobbys had never seen so many people crowded together. He was told that Edward's army totalled over 40,000 men, and that the Lancastrians assembling in the north had similar numbers. The next morning to the sound of trumpets and drums, the army decamped and headed north. After two hours watching the procession heading north, Hobbys was given instructions to follow. His was almost the last cart on the road. For several days they headed north, the weather getting colder and colder.

On the 28th March, having reached Yorkshire, the advance guard of Edward's army encountered some Lancastrians at Ferrybridge, the crossing of the river Aire. A minor battle there occurred resulting in a victory for Edward, and some wounded soldiers for Hobbys, though Hobbys surgical cart was too far behind the fighting men to be aware of the circumstances of the battle. The troops continued and as Hobbys arrived in the little village of Saxton, word spread down the ranks, that the main body of the Lancastrian army has been located, and that although the morrow was Psalm Sunday, the main battle would occur.

The next morning Hobbys awoke early in biting cold to sounds of trumpets organising the Yorkist army into a huge line, maybe a mile long and hundreds deep. Hobbys drew his wagon up half a mile behind the battle line to await developments and the arrival of wounded.

Snow began to fall heavily blotting out Hobbys view of the battlefield. Although sounds were muted, he could hear shouts, then the swishing noise of thousands upon thousands of arrows being released. No casualties arrived, no arrows fell near him.

More shouts and trumpets braying announced the main engagement, to be followed by the clash of steel on steel, shouts of victory and screams of agony. Hobbys could now just make out the huge body of soldiers ahead of him as the snowstorm abated. Wounded soldiers began to trickle back to Hobbys carried on stretchers. Hobbys was busy amputating, suturing, removing arrowheads, and for many just giving some pain relief till death provided merciful relief. One of Edward's priests joined Hobbys, and seemed just as busy providing final absolution. The battle noise continued, past midday and on and on as the faint sunlight began to dim.

Then Hobbys looking up from his work saw a mass of men to the right of the battlefield arrive and join the combat. They must be Norfolk troops arriving late, it was hard to find one's way in the heavy snowstorm. They crashed into the Lancastrian flank and within minutes the battle front began moving away from Hobbys, surely this must mean the Lancastrian line had broken and that Edward's army was in pursuit.

The advent of casualties slowed and night fell before messengers arrived back to say there would be few more wounded soldiers for Hobbys. The Lancastrians were throwing off their armour before fleeing and being chopped down from behind. Few were surviving, as Edward had ordered to give no quarter, and few Yorkists were getting wounded.

Hobbys walked over the battle field at sunrise to be greeted mostly by silence. He heard no moans and groans from wounded soldiers. Crows and dogs made the only noise he could hear as they fought over the corpses littering the ground. A few women scoured the field removing purses and gold teeth from the dead. It was clear that thousands upon thousands of the enemy had been killed, many while trying to escape. The Lancastrian leadership had not been spared. Lord Clifford, Henry Percy, Earl of Northumberland and Andrew Trollope had been killed, Henry Beaufort, the Duke of Somerset and Henry Holland, the Duke of Exeter had fled into exile. The old pious king Henry VI had been taken captive and Lancaster was destroyed as a force in the land. Edward's position on the throne was totally secure. Hobbys packed his wagon and headed back south to London

It was proposed to put poor old Henry VI in the Tower for the remainder of his days. Hobbys hoped he might get a chance to examine him to see if he could diagnose the cause of the king's attacks of melancholy and insanity. The Lancastrian doctors had failed to either ascertain the nature of the King's malady nor find a cause, but they had not had the benefit of as he did of a first class education and the devotion to his studies in Oxford.

Hobbys returned to Cambridge to continue his studies.

# WESTMINSTER PALACE JULY 1ST 1461

'Hobbys,' the guard roared, 'the king is ready to see you!'

Hobbys entered warily initially scanning Edward's face, there did not appear to be any anger, showing, thank God. He took in the man in front of him, even seated he was huge, he must have been a foot taller than anyone else in the room, his fair hair fell to his neck and his almost feminine blemish less visage was, well it would have appealed to men who like men, and probably appealed even more to the ladies. He was more striking, more – yes beautiful than all the reports he had heard. He radiated power and youthful vigour.

King Edward IV, as he was now proclaimed by right of both royal blood and battle, appeared entirely comfortable in the great hall of Westminster Palace, built on Thorney Island on the banks of the River Thames in central London. He occupied the elevated throne with elegant ease, the seat of power of English kings since the time of King Cnut over four hundred years ago before the disastrous Norman occupation.

Beside him stood a young man, and a boy perhaps age less than ten. Hobbys guessed them to be his two brothers, George, recently made the Duke of Clarence, and his little brother Richard, soon to become the Duke of Gloucester. Around him were other figures, some of whom Hobbys had seen before, William Hastings, knighted after Towton and the King's Chamberlain, William Herbert, the new Earl of Pembroke, and young Henry Stafford, new to Edward's court after the death of his grandfather, Humphrey, the first Duke of Buckingham at the battle of Northampton. Hobbys sank to his knees in front of the throne and looked at Edward's feet.

'Master Hobbys,' the king said, 'We believe you were briefly physician to my dear late father and my brother, the late Duke of York and the Earl of Rutland, so brutally cut down by the usurping Lancastrians.'

'Sire, I was but asked to take that role only the day before the battle at Wakefield.' Hobbys apologised.

'We understand from the surviving members of the Duke's court, that you advised him to await battle until I arrived with my army and that you were aware of the she-wolf of Anjou's perfidy in hiding troops and seducing John Neville to her side.' continued Edward.

'That is true your majesty, but he said I was hired for medical recommendations only, not military advice, and to curb my tongue,' apologised Hobbys again.

'Well Master Hobbys, your reputation as a doctor precedes you, but your skills as a councillor appear as valuable. I understand you still have a year to complete your doctorate at Cambridge University, but we have a plan for you after that. We are creating a new court position of Sergeant Surgeon, worth forty marks a year, with some allowance for food and drink, would you care to accept this position as one of my court physicians?' asked Edward.

Hobbys glowed internally. The Sergeant at Law was the highest position at the English Bar Counsel and Sergeant Surgeon would therefore be the highest surgical appointment in England requiring personal service to the king.

'Your Majesty, yes Your Majesty, such a position would be the greatest honour, I will care for all members of your court as requested to the best of my ability, thank you for honouring a humble physician with this responsibility.' gasped Hobbys.

Edward continued, 'Master Hobbys, we also thank you for attending the wounded last Psalm Sunday.'

'Your Majesty, it is an honour to serve the rightful king and his army. However, I must say that some more wounded soldiers and a few less frozen bodies would have helped keep me warmer at Towton. I searched the battlefield for survivors the next morning and found not one.'

'Master Hobbys, the Lancastrian front fought well for hours, allowing few survivors on either side, but once Jockey of Norfolk arrived on their flank, they provided less competition than the jousting quintain. Hopefully the country will enjoy some peace, pleasure and prosperity

for many years.' Edward observed Hobbys still on his knees.

'Get up man, did you know one of the benefits of this position is the privilege of drawing two "buttes of sacke" yearly from the royal cellars?'

'Your Majesty is most gracious'

'And,' continued Edward, 'another duty is supervising torture, to ensure the continued survival of traitors till they confess and swear allegiance.'

Hobbys blanched, imposing pain with treatment was inevitable, imposing pain for torture may contravene his Hippocratic Oath, however he would not be causing pain, only trying to limit that, and forty marks could help ease his anxiety and professional integrity.

'Your Majesty's wish is my command.'

Edward leapt up, 'Good, bring in young Henry Percy,' he ordered, and his guards escorted a sullen youth into the throne room, 'this young buck lost his father, the Earl of Northumberland, at Towton, and declines to swear allegiance to his rightful king. So Hobbys, I hear you are good at dissection, would you care to dissect this young man and demonstrate some anatomy to us?'

Hobbys looked at the youth whose arrogance was replaced with a look of fear. He looked back at Edward who gave him a wink.

'Your Majesty, I have not tried dissecting the living for a tutorial, it could be done, but I would need him to be tightly bound so he does not wriggle too much in pain under the knife, I would need him to be well gagged so my demonstration could be heard above his screams. The bleeding would be a problem, obscuring the field of vision, but a red hot cautery would stop that. My usual practice is to cut out the breast bone first, cutting it away from the ribs and collar bone. That takes about ten minutes, then having accessed the chest, I remove the heart, I regret to say that is a fatal step.'

There was a sound of retching as Clarence, Stafford and young Henry went pale and vomited. Interesting to note who the weak characters were in the room, not men you would rely on in difficulty thought Hobbys, so to it appeared that Edward made similar mental notes, casting a curious glance around the room. Richard, the only other person to note Edward's wink, had a quiet un-distressed smile on his face.

'Your Majesty,' squeaked Henry, 'I will swear allegiance to the House of York until…until I reach manhood, after that you will have to deal with me man to man.'

'Bravely said,' cried Edward, 'release the boy. Hobbys you are my man,' he said with another wink, 'you may go, my secretary will find you a room for your practice, and tell you more about the terms of your position.' Edward was bored with the topic, and hoped that was the last item of business for the day, as one of the court ladies had caught his eye, her smile back at the king did indeed terminate the day's business. Hobbys backed out gratefully to be conveyed to his rooms by one of Edward's clerks.

'Follow me.' said the clerk, 'So Hobbys, did you hear about Austragilda, wife of King Gontram of Burgundy, several hundred years ago? she had two royal physicians slain when she died and buried with her, to look after her in the next life. Make sure you look after the king and queen well, surgeons have been put to death when kings die on a battlefield!'

'As the king said, you have a bouge of court, a meat and drink allowance. You may keep any dressings from a royal wound, no doubt once cleaned and reapplied to one of your clients, it will have a higher cure rate and attract a higher fee. During any war, you are paid an extra ten pounds quarterly, plus ten pennies a day for expenses. You receive an allowance for expendables, and a fee of 180 pennies for dressing a dangerous or mortal wound. Not a bad job, eh Master Hobbys. Here we are, this is your room.'

Sitting in Hobbys room was his first visitor, his large swollen toe providing an obvious diagnosis. 'My dear physician, peace pervades the country, York is in control, now is a good time to sell your gold,' whispered Isaac the convert, still looking a little yellow.

# CAMBRIDGE NOVEMBER 1, 1461

Hobbys had completed his doctoral thesis entitled the 'An anatomical thesis, the evaluation and management of traumatic battlefield wounds'. The university professors were mostly impressed with his original studies during his final viva voce. Hobbys knowledge of anatomy was faultless, and his knowledge of the forefathers of medicine was comprehensive. His knowledge of theology however, had some gaps. He recalled the first five commandments well, but could not remember the last five in the correct order. He struggled to recite the seventh commandment while looking his examiner in the eye.

On the graduation day, all the doctoral candidates attired in scarlet gowns joined the academic procession to sit up on the stage. Hobbys hood of scarlet cloth lined with mid-cherry silk denoted his doctorate as medical science. They all wore voluminous velvet bonnets with a gold tassel.

Each doctoral candidate was presented to the chancellor of the university and the audience by the master of their college, a citation of their doctorate was read, and then each accepted the applause humbly. Hobbys glowed inside, few doctors in the land were as well qualified academically and practically as he. He surveyed the new graduates in the front rows, yes Argentine was there with a sour expression on his face. What a pleasure!

Then all the graduates passed over the stage briefly to shake hands with the chancellor, and receive their bachelor's degrees. Then the individual prize winners processed back on the stage for a second time to collect university medals. Hobbys self-congratulatory reverie was interrupted when John Argentine went back a fifth time, this time for the medical theology prize, one that had eluded Hobbys as an undergraduate graduate, and the professor of anatomy, dug Hobbys in the ribs to whisper that Argentine had won all the prizes and was the smartest physician in the university.

Hobbys seethed again, advising the professor that Argentine currently lacked practical experience and clinical judgement, and that time would tell how competent he was.

Hobbys dropped into the Eagle Tavern in St Benedict's Street, his favoured hostel in Cambridge, for a last drink of ale, or maybe two. The barmaids were not as hospitable as those he remembered in Oxford. On emerging a little unsteadily an hour later, he bumped into a gowned gentleman, dislodging a collection of books in the fellows arms. 'Forsooth,' he said, in what sounded a parody of the old king. They locked eyes, then both feigned uncertainty of the other's identity. 'Hobbys?' said the voice. 'Doctor William Hobbys to you, Argentine is it?'

'Yes that is I, I saw you getting a doctorate today didn't I? Something about chopping up battlefield casualties wasn't it?'

'It was pioneering work on battlefield wound management and causes of traumatic death, should you be able to progress to a doctorate, you will find it much more challenging that mere bachelor's degrees.' Hobbys replied, 'Yes I saw you on the stage joining us at the higher echelons of the University a few times.'

Argentine persisted, 'yes, I was blessed with some awards, one of which was the theology prize, which I was told eluded you during your bachelor's studies? Your reputation suggests you may have been busy with less biblical topics.'

Hobbys was incensed, but was also both impressed and unimpressed that his reputation had reached Cambridge. There were some bits he had hoped to leave in Balliol. 'I presume you are referring to my skills with the rapier, and becoming the Oxford University champion, perhaps you might like to have a few rounds with me, even a doctor needs more that an acid tongue to defend himself at time!'

Argentine bristled, 'Actually I thought you might like instead a game of chess as a more suitable challenge for two gentlemen of supposed higher intellect, rather than a swordfight more suitable for menial soldiers.'

Hobbys bridled and responded, 'we are both aware that chess is one of the knightly skills, but so are fencing, swimming and riding, archery, falconry and hunting riding, and even poetry or music. However I doubt if you aspire to knightly skills.'

Argentine froze briefly holding in his temper, he would lose should he engage in any form of combat with the stout pugnacious character before him. 'Ah knightly virtues,' he responded, 'I seem to recall that they include fidelity and nobility, your reputation suggests these are not important to you!'

They scowled at each other aware they would cross paths, usually hostile paths in future, they turned in their separate directions without another word, and left. He left Cambridge with none of the camaraderie that attended his departure from Oxford, and headed off to York to re-join the Royal Household now an experienced and highly qualified physician and surgeon.

# YORK NOVEMBER 19ᵀᴴ 1461

Hobbys as ordered, entered the royal bedroom to see the king resting on his bed, a lady partially hidden under the sheets but she did not have any visible clothing covering her shoulders. 'Hobbys!' roared Edward, 'I am sick, fix me up, we have bloody Lancastrians skulking in Alnwick, Bamburg and Dunstanborough Castles, the she-wolf of Anjou somewhere in the area with hundreds of damned French soldiers, and Warwick incapable of organising the sieges. We need to be out on the field, and,' he beckoned Hobbys closer to whisper in his ear, 'did you ever see a more tasty dish than this delectable wench, We are unable to satisfy her or our self, GET ME BETTER!'

Hobbys looked at the King and said, 'may I examine you, your Majesty,' Edward threw back the sheets to reveal two naked bodies; she was indeed a delectable dish. Hobbys looked quickly back at the king trying to keep his mind on professional matters; he was covered with a fine red rash all over. The king coughed and blew his nose, then rubbed his sore red eyes. Hobbys asked the king, 'Sire could you open his mouth for me?' Peering in at the inside of the cheeks Hobbys could see little spots like grains of salt.

'Your majesty,' he said with great self-importance, 'I regret to say you have measles, a simple infection that will settle in a few days if you rest alone.'

'However this was the cause of the Antonine plague which killed Emperor Lucius Verus, fourteen hundred years ago, when he would not rest alone. The spots are small and all over your body, but not on your hands and feet, you have red eyes and a cough and cold, and you have some tiny white spots inside your mouth, so I am pleased to say you do not have smallpox. The great Persian physician, Rhazes, was the first to describe the difference between the two diseases in his text The Book of Smallpox and Measles written about six hundred years ago.'

'Hobbys, 'begged Edward weakly, 'We are sure you are erudite and full of knowledge, but stop blathering man, we don't need a history lesson, GET ME BETTER!'

'Your Majesty, I will go back to my room immediately for some medication for you, which will make you better by next week. The condition is easily spread to other people, so I strongly advise you to sleep alone this week.' replied Hobbys.

Edward patted the lady on the rump and said, 'You heard the learned quack, run along, but come back next week so we really can have some fun. Hobbys, if I am better next week, you will become the principle surgeon of the royal body.'

Edward consumed Hobbys herbs dissolved in red wine. According to the young lady found in his bed, when she whispered discreetly in Hobbys ear a week later outside the royal bedroom, Edward was back to full strength. Three years then passed uneventfully without major medical disasters in the royal household or in the country, while Hobbys kept busy with the wealthier members of London society and their perceived ailments.

# FETTER LANE, JUNE 1462

Hobbys and his three sisters sat in the front lounge silently sipping on their wine glasses, all the guests attending his father's wake had left, many had been grateful patients for several years. Alice was busy clearing up in the kitchen. Hobbys read his father's will to the ladies. 'Father says all his books including Guido are to be sold to pay for his funeral, his bowl and pot are to go to his apprentice John Northorne, 6s 8p to the surgeon's college and 13s 4p to the barbers guild for food and drink, and he pardons my debt of twelve pounds loaned during my time in Oxford.' Good job his sisters did not know how much of that had been spent. 'His surgery here he leaves to me, and the remainder of his assets to be divided between you three.'

Hobbys was pretty sure that would not amount to much, as were his sisters who downed their wine, grabbed the unopened bottles and walked out. Hobbys reflected all was well with his life, his father had left him well provided with his qualifications and property, though he would miss there fireside chats over a glass of claret at the end of the day. Edward IV had just incorporated the barbers' guild into a company by royal charter, allowing it to supervise all other surgeons in London, following Hobbys petition to the king. Hobbys colleague Jacques Freis had assisted in the process, and both Edward and the young Duke of Gloucester were named as founders. Hobbys star was rising.

# 1462 SOUTHWARK

Hobbys emerged from the front door accepting grateful thanks from the family of man for whom Hobbys had performed surgery, it was dark and late. Hobbys, his reputation enhanced by his Doctorate at Cambridge, was now back working in the Yorkist Court, and also managing a large portion of his father's former practice. The hours were long and exhausting. The bells of the temple church struck eleven at night. Hobbys had yet to have his supper, yet he knew that Alice would be in bed, probably asleep, some cold food may be in the kitchen for him, but he would not have a welcome home at this hour.

'You poor man,' said a soft voice beside him, 'You must be in need of some food, drink and comfort, working so late.' Looking to his right was a petite young lady, with the bluest of blue eyes, blonde hair and the sauciest smile, standing in the next doorway. Hobbys thought she was correct, some food and drink would be very welcome. Accepting her offer, he followed through the door to a small room with a table and two chairs, she presented him with a goblet of wine, sat him down and disappeared through a door to return shortly with a loaf of bread, some cheese, several slices of beef pie and an apple. Was she offering an apple, could he be in the garden of Eden, or more likely the garden of unearthly delights. Hobbys ate and drank ravenously watching the young lady who sat maintaining eye contact while exposing half of her voluptuous breasts. 'So' she said, 'my name is Carole, what's yours?'

'Will.' he replied.

'So master Will, would you enjoy a little comfort as well?' Hobbys thought briefly, he had only been married six years, and had not strayed since his undergraduate years in Oxford, and, well yes, a bit during his time in Cambridge, but not in London. However, he was very tired and his guard was down. He had entirely forgotten poor Isaac the Converted's experience of the Southwark ladies of the night. His moral compass deflected partly by a long demanding day, but mainly by the euphoria of impending forbidden intimacy. He knew Alice would be asleep, and with only slight hesitation accepting her enticing offer and enticing body.

Carole led him through to the inner parlour where a steaming bath scented with rose petals had been prepared. The slowly removed her clothes, then his and helped him into the bath. First she washed his back, then his chest. Then she climbed into the bath and knelt across his thighs, at which point Hobbys was way past resisting any temptation.

As expected Alice was asleep and did not notice his arrival when he finally returned home. He had been paid a little more for his surgical expertise than he paid Carole for her most delightful hospitality. He took a mental note of her address, anticipating correctly that they would enjoy such intimate contact on many occasions in the future.

# MAY 1ST 1464 STONY STRATFORD

Hobbys was accompanying a royal hunt north of London, as injuries from misfortune with weapons to falls from a horse were not uncommon. He was sleeping soundly in the hunting lodge at Stoney Stratford having imbibed freely from one of his free buttes of sack from the royal cellar.

'Master Hobbys, sir, wake up, you must wakeup, the king wants you now!'

Hobbys rubbed his eyes wearily to see one of the King's pages beside his bed. 'The king needs you now, come quickly!' Hobbys pulled on his shirt, trousers and shoes, grabbed his medical bag and followed the earnest young man as he disappeared down the corridor to the royal bedchamber. Hobbys wondered what misfortune could have befallen the king, he was such a vital young man, with a gargantuan appetite for everything, perhaps he had an accident, fallen out of bed, attacked by a jealous husband, or perhaps one of his young lady's had caused a paraphimosis.

On arrival at the king's quarters he was greeted by Edward looking very healthy, dressed in his riding clothes and slapping his leg with a whip.

'Come on man, to horse, I need you as a witness, and I can think of no one in the palace more able to keep confidences.'

They rushed down the stairs out into the courtyard just after the sun had risen, where four horses saddled and ready awaited them, Edward's priest in his gown sat on one, and one of Edward's squires sat on the other.

'Forward,' shouted Edward and they rode of at a gallop as the devil was behind them. Hobbys wondered what on earth was this about, why did Edward need a priest and a physician? The only possibility he could think of was a duel, but who with, he seemed to have no enemies now, the Lancastrians were reasonably quiet, 'Oh God, oh no,' Hobbys thought, it will be a jealous husband, or even several of them knowing Edward's lustful appetite, He pursued with no discretion or discrimination the married and unmarried the noble and lowly: however, he took none by force, they just flocked to his bedchamber.

Suppose he is wounded or killed, oh my God, that will be bad for my practice! thought Hobbys, who would be King, George of Clarence, the next in line was only fourteen, a pretty boy of much vanity but little substance, young Richard was small and only what eleven? he thought, but there was so much determination and courage in that little body, and he loved his big brother so much, Edward had become a father figure to him. If only the old Duke of York has listened to him Rutland would still be here.'

Hobbys mused further, there was dotty old King Henry, still resident in the tower, and the boy Edward of Lancaster now ten, though everyone believed Somerset had fathered the child. Presumably the Lancastrians would emerge from the sewers to support them if Edward died, but there were all Edward's sisters as well, Anne, Elizabeth and Margaret, they had a child or two. Then that stupid woman Margaret Beaufort thought her son Henry was important in spite of coming from a couple of bastard lines. Hobbys father John had told him of the rumours going around when John was a boy, that of all the sons of Edward III, John of Gaunt had no resemblance to his father, or his brothers, and that it was suggested that he had been fathered by a Ghent butcher, certainly the

King had not attended his birth, and perhaps not his conception! That would make all the Lancastrians and Beauforts and Tudors illegitimate with no right to the throne of England. There really wasn't anyone to take over if Edward was killed in a duel. Perhaps I could fight for Edward as long as it is with rapiers, anything to stop this madness, concluded Hobbys.

After some five miles while Hobbys tried to develop a plan, they rode into the grounds of a large manor house, wheeled left and stopped in front of a small building, goodness it was a chapel, what was to happen.

'Dismount and follow me,' ordered Edward. As his eyes became accustomed to the darkness in the chapel, he saw two ladies standing at the altar. One was the most beautiful lady he had ever seen, tall, elegant, clothed in white, a wedding dress, with white blonde hair spilling over her shoulders, over her breasts. Her ice blue eyes locked with Edward's, she looked supremely happy, but there was also an indefinable trace of cold calculation. The other lady was older, similar, perhaps her mother. She had a compelling look in her eyes which were also locked on Edward.

Edward turned to the priest, 'Marry us now, we have adequate witnesses.' Hobbys gasped, so there was no duel, a wedding, a secret wedding without the approval of the king's council, while Warwick was in Savoy trying to find a suitable match for the king, this had trouble written all over it, again it might jeopardise his practice if his signature was on the marriage declaration.

'Your majesty, I...I...I, how can I do this, how do I know if either party has a previous betrothal, have the bans been read, I can't do this.' stammered the shocked priest. Obviously he also had not been informed of the reason for their early outing.

Edward held out a bag of money, and said, 'Would you like a large fee for this service?' then withdrew the bag to only hold it out again.

'God moves in mysterious ways.' replied the priest, accepting the offering and preparing for the service.

Edward turned to Hobbys and his squire, saying, 'You two are the official witnesses, you will sign the certificate, but say nothing to anyone about this.'

After A Brief Ceremony, Edward And His Beautiful Bride Kissed, She Sank To Her Knees, Extracted A Small Dagger From Her Garter Which She Held Out Handle First To Edward, Saying, 'I Do Not Think I Will Need This To Defend My Virtue Anymore.' Edward Accepted The Blade, Tossed It Aside With A Clatter On The Stone Floor With A Laugh, Then As The Ceremony Was Concluded, Edward Immediately Lifted The Lady To Her Feet, Hobbys Had Gathered Her Name Was Elizabeth From Their Vows, Ordered The Witnesses To Sign The Marriage Certificate, And Disappeared Out Of The Chapel Carrying His New Bride In His Strong Arms.

Hobbys Moved To Sign The Marriage Certificate Discovering The Bride's Name Was Elizabeth Wydville. Jogging His Memory, Hobbys Recalled That She Was The Widow Of A Sir John Grey Who Had Been Killed In The Second Battle Of St Albans Fighting, Fighting... For Henry Vi! There Would Be Hell To Pay When The King's Council Heard About This, She Was Clearly Not The Virgin Bride Required For Kings Having Already Had Two Sons, Oh Dear, This Really Could Damage His Practice.

Looking Again At The Certificate He Noted The Bride's Mother Signed As Jacquetta Wydville, Goodness, This Lady Was The Daughter Of The Count Of St Pol And Had Been Married To John Of Lancaster, The Late Duke Of Bedford, Uncle To Henry Vi. Well He Was Obliged To Sign It Hoping There Would Be No Adverse Outcome For Him, There Was Sure To Be For The King. The Small Wedding Party Stood Around Stunned Sharing Some Wine And Waiting.

Half-an-hour later Edward reappeared, breathless, dishevelled, smiling, accompanied by the beautiful Elizabeth, also a little tousled, with a deeply contented smile. 'Back to Stony Stratford.' he ordered, whereupon they mounted and rode slowly back, bemused by the event.

# WESTMINSTER ABBEY 26TH MAY 1465

Hobbys stood in the crowd at the back, wondering why as the royal physician, he was not allocated a seat nearer the front at least amongst the knights and gentry, if not the minor nobility. He could just see Elizabeth sitting on the throne, being crowned by the Archbishop of Canterbury, Thomas Bourchier, even from this far back she radiated a majestic ethereal beauty. She was flanked by Warwick and Clarence, Hobbys could not see their faces from the back, but they had been unsmiling as they walked into the abbey. Hobbys had been aware that many of the Queen's family had married or were betrothed into the old nobility, in spite of being seen as common upstarts by the likes of Warwick and Clarence. Earlier that year her brother John had been married to Katherine Neville, the old dowager Duchess of Norfolk when he was twenty and she was sixty-five! Hobbys had heard that Edward had forbidden Clarence to marry Isobel, Warwick's elder daughter. He had certainly seen George and Warwick whispering in dark corners around the palace recently.

However, the Queen had another brother Anthony Woodville, an interesting polite gentleman with a deep interest in medicine, after his travels around Arabia where he had read many fascinating books including Avicenna's Canon of Medicine. They had some absorbing discussions about the influence of Arabic medicine in England today. Hobbes thought he would have made a great physician; unfortunately, he seemed to be too tied up in being a minor aristocrat around the court.

Hobbys emerged from his thoughts when enthusiastic cheering broke out amongst the crowd as the newly crowned Queen walked back down the aisle, arm in arm with Edward, was there ever a more handsome couple on the throne of England?

# THE TOWER OF LONDON, AUGUST 1465

Hobbys surveyed the pathetic figure kneeling silently by his bed. Edward IV had asked Hobbys to check out the previous king, who had been discovered last month having a secret dinner with Sir Richard Temple at Waddington Hall near Clitheroe. His attempt to escape from there was unsuccessful. Henry, once King Henry VI, had been paraded through London, and was then confined to the tower, while Edward, now clearly master of his kingdom, celebrated with a Te Deum, a sermon and a procession to Thomas á Beckett's grave in Canterbury Cathedral.

The king had suggested it would be beneficial to find some morbid condition in the old king, one that might explain his death in the foreseeable future. Three physicians had seen him recently but had not reached a clear diagnosis or achieved a cure. Hobbys hoped he could succeed where John Arundel, John Faceby and William Hatteclyffe and a few surgeons had failed, that would be a feather in his cap, and help his practice. Hobbys was always keen to obey the king, but his Hippocratic Oath would prevent him from perjuring himself, as he congratulated himself on his integrity and professional virtue, he reflected that his medical principles were more potent than mere political whims.

'Your Grace,' called Hobbys, and again louder when he had no response, 'Your Grace, I am master Hobbys, physician to the king.........' he tailed off thinking that may not have been the best introduction.

Henry turned round looking somewhat vacant and confused. 'But I am the king, and I do not know you.'

'Your Majesty,' tried Hobbys again, 'I am your new doctor come to see if you are well.'

'Thank you master Hobbys,' said Henry, 'I am well, but why am I here, where are my courtiers and where is the queen, Margaret of Anjou. Where is the lad she says is my son, the one who looks so like Somerset?'

'Your majesty, please rest on the bed and allow me to examine you.'

Henry resigned himself and lay on the bed, while Hobbys surveyed his skin and mouth, laid his ear on Henry's chest at the back and front, felt the former king's abdomen for enlargement of the spleen or other organs, and checked his limbs for pain, deformity and power without finding any specific abnormality. He surveyed the chamber pot noting dark almost purple colour urine. Curious he thought, the late King Charles V of France, father of Henry V's queen, Catherine de Valois, grandfather of Henry VI, was reported to have developed the same thing when he went mad. This must signify some form of hereditary madness.

How he would impress his fellow physicians describing his skilled discoveries of rare diseases once a college of physicians was formed, Milan and Venice now had colleges of physicians, London should not lag behind. Once a new college, only for men like himself with bachelors' degrees and a doctorate for Oxford and Cambridge, was founded he could become a leading fellow, perhaps president! Argentine only had an MA in theology as his most eminent degree, and therefore would not be of a high enough standard for the presidency.

Then their intellectual superiority over the barbers and surgeons could be established, and all the unqualified quacks and women selling herbs could be thrown out of London. Unfortunately, both the king and the Duke of Gloucester had been honorary members of the barber-surgeons' guild since the year in which Hobbys had been Warden of the guild, and only saw a need for men to repair battle wounds rather than reach complex diagnoses though trained intellect. He could become the Avicenna, the Gaddesden, of this century. Hobbys thought he must find time to write a new text of medicine.

Hobbys thought he could not yet decide how to inform the king, while maintaining his ethical principles, and not admitting that he did not know what was wrong with Henry, some new form of purple melancholia, yes that sounded an impressive diagnosis, he would say that to Edward.

# LONDON 1465-1471

A few more years passed. Edward and Elizabeth had three daughters, Elizabeth in 1466, Mary in 1467 and Cecily in 1469, but so far he lacked a son and heir. Hobbys assisted at the deliveries, but Elizabeth needed little help, she produced children like shelling peas. Every birth Edward was delighted, and showered his wife with gifts, before seeking another new lady to bed. Edward and Warwick progressively drifted apart, Neville sought an alliance with France, Edward with Burgundy, Warwick's brother George Neville was removed from the office of Chancellor and the Woodville faction grasped more and more power in the council.

John Clerk was the king's apothecary, and blended the herbs and spices as prescribed by Hobbys and the other physicians. Poor John was never paid by Edward for his services, though the king granted him exemption from custom on his medications and other goods shipped through the Port of London. John was also apothecary for Katherine Neville, the king's aunt and subsequently also his sister in law following her marriage to the queen's brother John, even though she was forty-six years older than him. Poor John had to take Katherine to court to obtain his reasonable fees. Hobbys was glad that his personal contact with his patients increased the probability of being paid for his services.

Hobbys continued his practice in Holborn with occasional visits to the Place of Westminster depending on which other members of the Royal family were present and in need of his services. Some of the king's other physicians supervised Edward's meals and other minor medical issues.

Roger Marchall, another royal physician with an MD from Cambridge, had regular discussions with Edward about his diet. The king had recently developed some erroneous ideas about a nutritious diet from the McDonalds. Negotiations for a treaty with John McDonald, the Scottish Lord of the Isles had led to Edward temporarily favouring a Scottish diet of offal. Haggis they called it, encased in two slices of wheat bun, washed down with Scottish whisky, which did not meet with medical approval from either Marchall or Hobbys. Hobbys found the Haggis caused severe nausea, even if he did not think about its contents, and the whisky, the water of life apparently was what the Scots called it, burnt his throat violently. Adverse events soon inhibited this culinary style favoured by the king.

Clarence, a handsome shallow populist was easy pickings for Warwick. Clarence was greedy for power and riches, and incurably jealous of his brother. Warwick's offer of the throne appealed to his vicious discontented nature. Warwick raised troops and arranged the marriage of Clarence to his eldest daughter, Isabella in Calais; Edward underestimated the severity of the risings around him. He thought the rebellion would be easily suppressed, failed to assemble an army of adequate size, and his small force was defeated at the battle of Edgecote. Edward was captured and imprisoned by Warwick in Warwick Castle in July 1469. Warwick ordered the execution of the Queen's father, Richard Wydville, Lord Rivers, and the Queen's brother John Wydville.

Again a noble holding the king captive had inadequate authority to run the country, especially when hostilities on the Scottish Border required an organised response. Edward regained control of the government, and Warwick and Clarence fled overseas. They returned with an army and Margaret of Anjou in a turnaround of alliances. Then Edward escaped with his younger brother, Richard of Gloucester, to gather another army and returned to do battle for his throne and kingdom. Anonymous letters were slipped under Hobbys door keeping him informed of the revolving doors of power in Westminster, with the usual advice on when to buy and sell gold. Sometimes a fine bottle of French wine was tucked inside the front door. A message clearly from a different source also informed him of the queen's pregnancy, and when his services would be required. Loyalties were best concealed as the allegiances of London gangs fluctuated.

During Edward's brief exile, Elizabeth Wydville took herself into sanctuary in Westminster Abbey. On 2nd November 1470, her first son was born, aided by Lady Scrope and old mother Cobb, the sanctuary midwife. Hobbys observed the birth, but his surgical skills were unrequired.

Edward entered London again on 11th April 1471, and Elizabeth was able to emerge from sanctuary and return to the Place of Westminster where she was able to present the king with his first son, also named Edward. Edward spent the night with his family in Baynard's Castle. He summoned Hobbys to check the health of his wife and young family, informing the surgeon that he would be accompanying Edward, Gloucester and all their supporters and troops on the morrow as he would be finding some work for Hobbys skills.

Edward planned to strike Warwick's forces before Margaret of Anjou arrived with a second army, Clarence, his false ephemeral brother had been seduced back into the family fold with promises of riches and titles as well as persuasion that family blood ties were more important than anything in life or death. Battle lines were drawn up on the night of the 13th April in thick fog at Barnet. Edward deliberately camped close to Warwick's front line. He ordered that camp fires would only be lit a mile behind his actual line, so the desultory cannon fire through the night passed overhead and landed well past his troops.

# BARNET 14 APRIL 1471

Edward commenced battle early in the morning while the fog was still extremely dense. After an hour's fighting Hobbys peered through the gloom, suspecting that the front lines had swung though ninety degrees, his sword still sheathed, grateful that the battle front had not swung the other way in the fog to include his cart bearing a few wounded soldiers and his battle field equipment. Hobbys thick gown of musterdevillers, with a beaver hood left to him by Rowland Frankysshe, a barber-surgeon friend and colleague last month, kept him warm, and the grey colour made him less visible in the thick fog.

Hearing a clash of arms and shouts of traitor coming from nearby in front of him in thick fog, he walked cautiously forward and was surprised to see dimly men emblazoned with star and rays badge of John de Vere, the Earl of Oxford, engaged in battle with the forces of John Neville, the Marquis of Montagu, yet both had started that morning in the forces of Lancaster. King Edward must have persuaded one of these men to change sides.

Another hour passed with the clash of arms, the battle cries of soldiers, and the screams of pain from the dying and mutilated soldiers, before the noise started to abate. Hobbys advanced again seeking casualties, as few had been carried back to his cart, and information of the state of the battle. Often fully fit men were engaged exclusively in combat, and there were none left to convey the fallen back for medical assistance. A huge man leaning on his blood stained sword and wearing the three leopards on his tunic below a gold crown on his head appeared as he searched through the chaos and miasma of the battle which had just finally ceased as Warwick's men threw down their weapons.

'Your Majesty, I am here to ensure that you have emerged from the battle unscathed, though indeed it was hard to find you in this fog. You appear in better shape than the Earl of Warwick lying there" said Hobbys looking around.

'Master Hobbys,' welcomed Edward,' you find me excellent well, a little sport before breakfast is admirable for the appetite, however I can see my brother of Gloucester bleeding from his battle-axe arm. Young Richard in his first battle has clearly won his spurs, God's blood Dickon, your ferocious charge at Warwick's left wing turned the battle, what courage, what fighting, you were lucky to have only a superficial wound, you know Hobbys, his two esquires, John Milwater and Sir Thomas Parr were slain on either side of him, trying to protect Richard,'

Richard smiled, pale, exhausted but deliriously happy to be victorious beside his brother in arms. 'Francis Lovell and Richard Ratcliffe stood beside me then and kept most blows off me, but this bleeding is making a mess of my clothes Hobbys.'

'Sire, allow me to see your arm.' begged Hobbys, 'your courage in battle is commendable, but you are bleeding through the armour.' Richard pulled of his arm plates and glove to reveal a deep gash spurting blood over his upper arm. Hobbes applied pressure for a few minutes. 'Your Grace that looks very painful, allow me to give you an inhalation of pain relief, the soporific sponge has been soaked in a mixture of opium, mandrake juice, hemlock and henbane diluted with some water before I repair your wound.' suggested Hobbys. Richard looked at him doubtfully, and said, 'Master Hobbys, I appreciate your concern, but the only pain I feel is for my mentor and cousin, the Earl of Warwick, how sad that events should have come to a battle and his death. Master Hobbys, I understand that your dwale can lead to not only to the sleep of no pain, but the sleep of death. Pray proceed without your herbs.'

Edward and his retinue withdrew briefly, leaving surgeon and patient alone. The battle hardened warriors had little stomach for surgical needles.

Hobbys sutured the edges of the wound tight together with his finest needle and gut while Richard watched the repairs stoically. 'Well Hobbys, this wound will heal well, but I will be left with a deeper knife wound, beyond your powers to heal, a spirit wound, a deep grief that my mentor, my dearly loved substitute father should betray the house of York and now lie dead, and that my brother George, fickle George, should briefly betray the king. Can we ever trust him again, I wonder,' Richard said softly, sadly.

Edward re-entered as the procedure was completed, peering at the carefully approximated wound edge. He held a silver gilded ring emblazoned with an image of a bear and ragged staff, the emblem of Richard Neville, the dead traitorous Earl of Warwick. 'Dear brother, we took this from Warwick's hand. I would like you to keep it as a memento of happier days when you were squire to one of the great warriors of our day, our dearest cousin and supporter of the house of York, as a memento of your first battle when you won your spurs with incredible courage, and sadly as a reminder of the fate of all traitors.'

He slipped the ring on Richard's hand, while casting a surreptitious look at Clarence to see his reaction to that statement. Clarence surveyed the ground, showing no evidence of hearing Edward.

Hobbys spoke to Gloucester, 'Your Grace, allow me to press hard on this bandage for ten minutes, it should then heal rapidly, but I advise you to avoid battle for a month,'

Edward laughed. 'So Master Hobbys, will you tell the she-wolf of Anjou that your Lord of Gloucester has been inconvenienced, and would be grateful if she could delay her landing till June.'

Richard laughed as well. 'A mere scratch will not deprive me of the pleasure of dispatching the next Lancastrian army, including Edward of Lancaster, when it has the temerity to show its face. A little exercise in the front rank will hasten healing Master Hobbbys, thank you I am grateful for your treatment.'

Edward looked speculatively at his brother, 'So Dickon, who do you think fathered that traitor? Remember William Ayscough, the Bishop of Salisbury, no you were not born when he was beheaded, but he was Henry VI's confessor. It is said that he swore the saintly king to a life of celibacy, our father always thought Edward Beaufort, Duke of Somerset was a more likely father.'

'Either way, he will not be with us much longer!' growled Richard.

Edward laughed at his brother's youthful ferocity, 'Dickon, my court bard will pen some lines about your heroism'. A few days after the battle a court poet compared Richard's valour to Hector of Troy with a few lines: -

> *The Duke of Gloucester, that noble prince*
> *Young of age and victorious in battle*
> *To the honour of Hector that he might come*
> *Grace him followeth, fortune and good speed....*

Watching all this bloodied martial glory, Hobbys wondered about his reward for his service, had not William Hatteclyffe, the King's last physician, then his secretary, been rewarded with estates in Oxfordshire, London and Somerset only four years ago? Hobbys wondered idly why the King's secretary was esteemed and paid more by the monarch than his physician, after all it did not take three years of dedicated study in a top university to become a mere secretary, and Hatteclyffe had studied in Cambridge which was nearly as venerated as Hobbys alma mater. Mind you it was reputed that William had loaned the king eighty pounds and not been repaid for years.

Hobbys reveries were disturbed by the sight of a corpse beside him. The naked body appeared to belong to a young man with flowing blond hair. Hobbys could not see a mark on the body and wondered how he may have died, he appeared a good subject for a post-mortem. His weapons, armour, boots and clothing had been stripped of the body. There was blood on his lips and gum, perhaps where a gold plated tooth has been pulled out. Such is life, Hobbys thought, once overtaken by death on the battlefield, possessions become the public property of the survivors. He could not even tell if the man had died fighting for the Yorkists or Lancastrians. His body now was Hobbys' possession; no soldier would have any more interest.

Hobbys had the body carried to his cart and brought out his medical equipment. A superficial survey revealed only a large bruise on the left temple, where presumably he had been hit by a right handed opponent wielding some heavy weapon. The bone felt fractured, but not displaced. There was otherwise not a mark on the body. Hobbys thought the inside of the body would reveal some interesting secret. He opened up the abdomen as usual, and found all the internal organs to be intact, there was no blood to be seen. Hobbys cut out the breastbone in the usual fashion, and peered inside the chest, again all organs appeared intact with no blood or lacerations. On removing the heart, he was surprised to find the heart and major vessels were empty of blood, most odd he thought, there is no evidence of any bleeding, yet there is no blood in the heart. That appeared one of the many mysteries he experienced when performing post-mortem examinations. He would present these findings to the next guild meeting where he would expect some praise, no, a lot of praise, for his observations, and perhaps some discussion on possible causes of this surprising discovery.

Soldiers passing yelled some ribald comments at Hobbys, 'Hungry work was it master surgeon, found any good bits to eat'. One peered in any said in disgust, "Oooh yuk, that looks revolting'. Hobbys was left to continue his work. Approaching the corpse from behind the head, he sliced through the skin from just behind one ear, over the mastoid bone, up over the top of the head, and down the other side. He picked up the scalp and slowly dissected it forwards, off the bone to the forehead just above the eyes, and then the posterior flap of the scalp back of the bone to the back of the neck, leaving most of the skull bone exposed.

He picked up his saw and cut down through the skull bone following the line of his original incision, careful to angle the blade to cut through bone, but no deeper than that. Then he sawed through the skull in a horizontal plane from the back of the skull, known as the occiput. When the two cuts met at right angles, he was able to lift off a part of the skull, revealing the posterior half of the brain. More surprises were in store, there was a large amount of blood in the right side of the brain, squashing the cerebral hemisphere, and when Hobbys elevated the occipital lobe to look at the rear lower portions of the brain, parts of the cerebellum and stem of the brain were apparently forced through the foramen magnum, the hole at the base of the skull where the brain connected with the spinal cord.

What did this mean, wondered Hobbys, there wasn't enough blood in the skull to cause death from blood loss, so why was the heart empty of blood, perhaps the deformity of the brain caused death, and some sort of spinal reflex caused by brain damage emptied the heart. Hobbys thought it was most unusual. This would be a good case to present to the guild, his colleagues should be extremely impressed. Lost in thought he didn't even notice a couple of dogs roaming over the battle field grab the heart and liver from his pile of dissected internal organs and disappear for a good meal.

Hobbys replaced the skull flap, pulled the two flaps of scalp back into place, and sutured the scalp and trunk skin flaps back together, before getting one of his assistants to wheel the corpse off to the mass grave just dug.

# TEWKSBURY, MAY 4TH 1471

After the Battle of Barnet, Margaret and Somerset landed at Weymouth and planned to join up with the Welsh army Jasper Tudor was raising. However; after the Lancastrians were refused entry into Gloucester, and forced marches by both armies, Edward caught up with his sworn enemies at Tewksbury. Hobbys watched from behind the lines with concern as the king ordered, ready to attend casualties. His rapier by his side looking rather pathetic compared to the soldier's heavy battle swords.

The Lancastrians had the higher ground south of the town, and between them was very uneven ground, with a network of foul lanes, deep dykes and high hedges making a frontal attack extremely difficult. Hobbys thought it was as evil a place for a battle as he had ever seen. Edward as always was undeterred, his confidence and courage, Hobbys thought would enable him to tear down the gates of hell!

Edward commanded his main force in the centre, while Richard commanded the vanguard on the left opposite Somerset's right flank, and Hastings commanded the right. Edward's artillery and archers commenced the battle causing such destruction on Somerset troops, that he ordered a counter-attack, a charge at Edward's central battle line. His attack included some men who attacked Edward's flank after approaching hidden by lanes and hedges leading to some violent hand-to-hand fighting. However, Richard's van turned to Edward's aid, and some 200 men hidden in the neighbouring wood on the left flank also out flanked Somerset's troops. The Lancastrians crumbled and fled, then Edward turned his whole line of battle on Prince Edward of Lancaster's division destroying the remnant of the Lancastrian Army.

Hobbys busied himself again with suturing and binding many wounds as the less serious injuries filtered back through the lines. He was relieved to see Richard and Edward embrace once the fighting ceased apparently uninjured this time.

Prince Edward was slain endeavouring to flee, and then begging for mercy, many leading Lancastrians were captured and beheaded on the battle field, those who sought sanctuary in Tewksbury Abbey including Somerset was were dragged out, and after a brief trial directed by Richard and Norfolk, were beheaded in the market place.

Hobbys sat outside the Olde Black Bear once the battle and post battle executions were over, he could hear very loud revelries from inside where the eminent members of the Yorkist army were celebrating their success. Not for the first time, he wondered why he had not been asked to join in as the senior doctor to the Yorkist nobility. Nevertheless, his pint of ale and pigeon pie were very welcome after the hot work of the day.

His quiet sojourn was disturbed by the approach of a laden cart driven by two of Edward's soldiers and surrounded by an entourage of other men at arms wearing the white boar of Gloucester. They stopped opposite Hobbys table and the sergeant called to him,

'Master Hobbys, we have brought you your reward by special order of my Lord of Gloucester for your valour this day!' Raucous laughter broke out from the soldiers. 'Guess what we have for you here under this canvas, Hobbys, specially ordered by the Duke 'oo knows what thee likes?'

Prospects of gold and silver from the Lancastrian treasure wagon went through Hobbys head, no less that he deserved for fixing Gloucester's arm so he could fight today. At that one of the soldiers pulled back the covering to reveal a pile of dead bodies, covered in blood, many with severe obviously fatal wounds, but no treasure.

'My Lord of Gloucester says thee likes to chop 'em up, to be sure they are dead, are they tasty master surgeon, I think I would rather your ale and that pie!' More laughter followed from the soldiers, eager for some entertainment with some ales.

'Just for a bit of variety for you we picked up the body of a poor little boy lying by the road, and we cut down one of the Lancastrians 'oo had just been hung from that tree across the road, so 'oos a lucky man then, are you going to say thank you, 'ow about showing us what you do then?' continued the sergeant.

'Yer, shows us some guts and other bits!' called one of the soldiers, as the others fell about with hysterical laughter, no doubt fuelled by the relief of surviving today's butchery, and by the first few ales from Gloucester.

Hobbys was torn between being the centre of attention and the lack of respect for his skills being shown by the soldiers. Recognising the need to provide some entertainment, he looked at the pile of dead bodies. The poor little boy looked emaciated, his gums were swollen and had been bleeding, most of his teeth had fallen out, and his breastbone was surrounded by a vertical row of bony knobs where the ribs joined the breastbone, all known signs of inadequate food, but not much of fun to show out of control soldiers.

The unfortunate who had just been hung was more likely to provide some fun, Hobby downed the remainder of his ale and pigeon pie, and asked the soldiers to put the body on the trestle table in front of the Olde Black Bear. It was the most unusual place he had ever done a post mortem, he hoped the guild of barber-surgeons would not be upset. He covered the body with a large cloth, pulled out a knife and cut off the man's trousers under concealment, finding what he had suspected, a frequent finding after hanging. Turning to the men, he said, 'What do you think we will see here?' They all crowded around as Hobbys whipped of the cloth to reveal a very dead man with blue lips and a huge erection! Well that was the perfect show for the soldiers, more hysterical laughter followed accompanied by ribald comments about whether that would be needed where he was going or not, and bringing out the 'ladies of the pub' to give him a good send off. They even offered to pay for the service for him.

Hobbys thought enough levity, time to show his expertise. He waved away the unfortunate condemned man, and pointed to one of the more blood stained corpses on the cart. 'That one next,' he ordered. The man was placed on the pub table and various body fluids leaked onto the timber that usually carried food and drink. The odour around the group rapidly became offensive, and a few of the men retched and headed inside.

'Cut off all his armour and clothes,' Hobbys ordered. Once naked, the extent of his injuries became apparent, he had lost his right hand, his left leg below the knee and had a huge abdominal wound just to the left side though which some blood and smelly brown liquid was seeping. While he may have survived the injury to his arm, death from shock and blood loss would have ensued fairly rapidly from either of the other two lesions. His pain would have been severe but brief. His skin appeared extremely pale. Hobbys carefully cut down the middle of the abdomen to the pubic bone. The abdomen fell open; loops of intestine emerged covered in blood and excreta, and there were pools of blood throughout the abdominal cavity. Hobbys found a section of lower bowel cut open by the final fatal injury, or at least one of them, with a large incision almost cutting right across the colon, and a large slash in the spleen, which would have caused most of the bleeding. He dissected out the bowel, liver, spleen and kidneys and piled them up on the table as the number of soldiers diminished leaving a few gaping at the internal organs in awe of Hobbys surgical skill.

Having done that, Hobbys turned his attention to the chest. He separated the ribs on both sides from where they joined the breastbone, which he then removed, allowing the chest wall to gape open, allowing a clear view of the heart and lungs. He made two little nicks in the front of the heart and inserted his fingers to get a better grasp of this organ, than slipped his hand behind to pull it forward such that he could disconnect the heart from the major vessels to which it was attached. He placed the heart on the table next to the sergeant's second pint of ale, tipped a little of the fluid over it to wash off some blood and grime, then slipped his knife into the apex and opened up the wall of the heart. Inside he was curious to note the absence of any blood within the heart or great vessels. He could understand that in this case the finding was due to blood loss from his injuries, but why he found an absence of blood in the heart of great vessels in other corpse who had died only with a head wound without severe bleeding from multiple wounds remained a mystery.

His thoughts were interrupted by an irate publican emerging from the front, to find bits of body where guests with food and drink should be. The publican had surveyed the bits of human offal wondering if they could be included in his sausage mix, but Hobbys threw them back inside the corpse, and sutured the skin together with a few large stitches. The few remaining voyeurs or perhaps true scientists amongst the soldiers threw the corpses back on the cart, tipped some buckets of water over the table washing off blood, gore and excrement which was then mixed by soldiers' boots into the dirt and horse excrement, and took the bodies off to the mass grave that had been dug on the edge of town, while the sergeant took Hobbys inside for another ale as thanks for the demonstration, which turned out to be not as hilarious as they had thought initially.

Margaret of Anjou was captured a few days later to be imprisoned in the Tower, her spirit finally broken, as was the Lancastrian cause which appeared dead and buried with no legitimate claimant to the throne. England finally seemed at peace with the wars all over

# 21ST MAY 1471

Seventeen days after the battle, Henry VI died in the tower, according to official sources he died of displeasure and melancholy on hearing of the battle of Tewksbury, the death of his son and the imprisonment of his wife. Apparently the three sons of York had all been present in the tower that night. The next day, his body was displayed at St Paul's cathedral with his face exposed so all could see the king was dead. The public were surprised to see blood dripping down from the skull. From there the body was placed on display at Black Friars, and then by boat to Chertsey Abbey for burial. As usual Hobbys was permitted to see the body, though in this case not to perform an autopsy. Hobbys noted the back of his skull was coated with blood and the bone was broken in several palaces, it felt soft and the pieces crunched against each other when Hobbys pressed on the back of his skull. Perhaps the poor old man had fallen over, but more likely someone had taken a club to his head! The old king was left with only a few well-worn teeth, the right lower jaw had no residual teeth, but there were no signs of recent trauma to the jaw. The right upper arm was red and swollen with an abscess near the shoulder. Hobbys touched it lightly with his knife, at which point it discharged some foul smelling pus. Hobbys probed the wound finding the infection involved the bone, which broke under his gentle examination. Hobbys felt the smell would be too awful during a royal funeral, and the now flail arm would flop about and possible even fall off, so he dislocated the shoulder, and removed the right arm. Otherwise the body appeared intact with no new clue as to why he lost his wits intermittently, though Hobbys was interested to note the Henry had very small atrophic testes, perhaps the rumours of childhood mumps were true. Henry could then not have fathered Edward of Lancaster! He then wrapped the body up carefully in the hope that his surgery would not be noticed, and disposed of the arm in a rubbish bin on his way out.

# WESTMINSTER ABBEY 11TH JUNE 1471

Following the death of Henry VI and Edward, Prince of Lancaster, Edward was feeling finally secure on his throne. He had his son Edward, now aged seven months, created Prince of Wales, then on 3rd July the great nobles of the land gathered in Westminster Palace to swear to acknowledge Edward as true and undoubted heir to our sovereign lord, as to the crowns and realms of England and of France and the lordship of Ireland. Hobbys had been asked to check the boy's health before the event, but was somewhat disappointed and surprised not to be asked to the official ceremony.

# WESTMINSTER PALACE 1473

E dward sat on his throne, yawning intermittently as the day's official business was discussed, the finances did not seem as interesting as the young lady carrying wine around his advisers, however he became aware that one of his ministers was complaining about royal expenditure. 'Of course bloody wars are expensive, tell all the treacherous Lancastrians!' Edward roared at his ministers, 'We can't afford to antagonise everyone or it will be on again, take some more estates from some of the traitors, but no, you can't reverse grants to men who have supported us through the difficult times in the past. Hobbys, our trusty and well beloved servant, chirugeon for our body, saviour of our brother Gloucester at Barnet is definitely exempted from any reduced grants! Did you not read our recipe for preventing and curing plague? We wrote that two years ago in common English for our people, with the assistance of Master Hobbys.'

# 17<sup>TH</sup> AUGUST 1473, FETTER LANE

Hobbys was busy attending the wealthy citizens when another thunderous knock on the door was expected to announce a summons to the palace. A dusty sweaty messenger wearing the royal livery of three leopards, and leading a second horse announced that the queen was due within a week and Hobbys was to come immediately as the queen was in Shrewsbury! Hobbys now kept a spare bag of surgical tools in his room in the palace and a second by the front door to be prepared for any dramas that befell Edward. They seemed to occur with monotonous regularity! So after asking his clerk to apologise to his morning patients and cancel the list for a week, he leapt into the saddle, and followed his guide at a gallop through London to the north-west. After two nights in hostelries and frequent changes of horses in post houses they arrived in the old city of Shrewsbury. Hobbys guide had given him little rest, having been informed by Edward that Hobbys would never father another child, or enjoy similar pleasures if he did not arrive in time.

Shrewsbury was an old market town known for its wool and brewing, Hobbys was pleased to recall. He would be entitled to a few celebratory ales after the birth! Why the king should choose to be here at the time of a royal birth surprised Hobbys. It was the fourth largest city in England and the site of many skirmishes with the Welsh. Henry IV and Harry Hotspur had fought here seventy years ago, but the place seemed peaceful enough at the moment. Perhaps Edward intended that it should remain so.

When Hobbys entered the royal apartment in the castle he found Elizabeth was looking fairly tranquil as her lady-in-waiting and two midwives fussed over her. The midwives told Hobbys that all was progressing well and that he could wait outside, to be called in the event of serious problems. Hobbys could see the queen clutching a piece of red jasper, according to pagan superstition it was known as the stone of endurance, it brought energy and a calm determination to overcome pain during childbirth. Well thought Hobbys, no harm in getting all the help possible, good job the priest was outside the room, unlike Westminster Palace where they seemed in plague proportions always tutting in disapproval at Hobbys.

The ladies-in-waiting were muttering prayers to St Margaret of Antioch, said to be the patron saint of childbirth. That poor St Margaret was beheaded at the age of fifteen still a virgin. Hobbys couldn't see much fun in that, though her father was reputed to have been a pagan priest, that sounded much more fun with all the old fertility rites. The thought of an emergency caesarean section to save the life of a royal prince, but would almost certainly kill the mother filled him with anxiety, but that was what surgeons had to do when a queen was labouring. Princes were more difficult to replace than wives was how Warwick had put it to him once. However as with her previous berthing's, the procedure passed fairly rapidly and uneventfully in the hands of the midwives. Elizabeth made it look as easy as shelling peas producing a perfect healthy baby with a problem-free labour. The cry of a lusty son brought Edward to her side where he was delighted to kiss Elizabeth and cradle his second son in his arms. Hobbys returned to Fetters Lane almost unnoticed.

Hobbys having been present at the birth, attended the christening of the infant Richard of Shrewsbury in Westminster Abbey. Thomas Bourchier, the Archbishop of Canterbury, himself a descendant of Edward III, supervised. Hobbys, Edward and Elizabeth proudly checked the royal infant before the ceremony, pronouncing him to be in perfect health. Queen Elizabeth sat beside her husband, both enthroned at the front of the Abbey. She looked totally satisfied and in control.

Hobbys wondered if she played chess. She would be a master of long term strategy, while Edward would play an aggressive game with an all-out attack, aiming to capture the queen as quickly as possible, then loose interest if the game was prolonged.

Elizabeth had installed herself as the white queen, the most powerful piece on the board, and in control of the King's love if not his lusts. Her elder brother Anthony Wydville, the second Earl Rivers and Governor of the Prince of Wales household, was one of her castles. Her son, Edward, Prince of Wales, and heir to the throne was her other castle. Her two sons, by her first marriage, Thomas, the first Marquess of Dorset, and Richard, soon to be knighted according to rumour, were her knights. She was also planning an eminent career in the church for her brother, Lionel, a potential bishop. She had marginalised Edward's brothers, Gloucester and Clarence, to the role of minor pawns, a very minor pawn in George's case.

On the other side of the board, the black king, Henry VI, and the black queen, Margaret of Anjou were removed from the board. Warwick, the dominant black castle was gone, as was Edward of Lancaster, the other black castle. Two black knights, the Dukes of Suffolk and Somerset were dead. There were few opposition pieces left. Elizabeth probably saw Clarence as a black piece to be removed one of these days.

Clearly Elizabeth Wydville was a dangerous opponent, an expert in the chess board of life, Hobbys concluded. Perhaps she would give Argentine a few lessons, Hobbys would be delighted to see him loose.

# FETTER LANE 1474

A young man with a familiar appearance entered Hobbys surgery. He introduced himself as Jacob and complained of blood and pus in his urine with painful urination. He admitted to visiting the ladies of Southwark. Hobbys prescribed the usual mixture of wine, oil, and vinegar to be taken twice daily, and making a guess about Jacob's physiognomy, also recommended oil of balsam, the traditional Hebrew Balm of Gilead endorsed by Hippocrates, to be applied to Jacob's member now and after visits to Southwark. If applied before it would considerably reduce the period of exposure to infection owing to the discomfort experienced by the ladies of Southwark!

Then Jacob further introduced himself as Jacob the Converted, the son of Isaac. 'my poor father died a few years ago, he told me he had been poisoned by the French, he also told me to bring the latest news to you as you cared for him so well. My sources in the court say that a treaty, a forty-five-year truce, will shortly be signed by King Edward and James III of Scotland. Richard of Gloucester as the king's representative has gone to Fotheringhay, his birth place, to meet the Scottish envoys. Princess Cecily will be betrothed to young Prince James with a dowry of twenty thousand marks to be paid in instalments every February at the Edinburgh Cathedral of St. Giles.

But you know what this means, you know why Edward did this? It leaves his northern border secure so he can launch an invasion of France next year. It means war with France.' Jacob's voice dropped to a conspiratorial whisper just like his father, 'Master Hobbys, the king will be looking for taxes, now is a good time to buy gold which we can keep secretly and securely for you, before the treasury searches your coffers and the price of gold goes up again!'

Hobbys looked in amazement. 'How do you know all this, surely your sources would be recognised as being, er well not English and thrown out of the palace?'

Jacob continued in his whisper, 'Master Hobbys, our existence has been precarious in London for centuries, we keep ourselves well prepared by being well informed, but I can't tell you how.'

# PHYSICIANS MEETING JUNE 1475

Hobbys entered the meeting room to disapproving looks from all round the room. 'So Hobbys,' said Robert Halyday, one of Hobbys colleagues, sounding very virtuous, 'master of the barber-surgeons' guild, do you know I was called to Southwark a few days ago to suture some men injured in a fight in a brothel along with Thomas Rolf. On looking into the next cubicle who should I see but the King's doctor naked in bed with a young lady of the establishment, and they weren't reading Gaddeston's medicine. Such behaviour will bring our profession into disrepute, and the guild will have to take some action if this behaviour is repeated.'

Bloody hell, though Hobbys, the king does this every day and gets away with it, why not his doctor? 'Can we get on with the main professional items on the agenda, and avoid tittle-tattle,' responded an embarrassed Hobbys.

# WESTMINSTER 1475

Two days later Hobbys was summoned to Westminster for an audience with the king. Surely he will not criticize me for a little levity when off duty, Edward does this all the time, hoped Hobbys.

Edward was throned in splendour in the Great Hall, Elizabeth was sitting beside him on her throne, looking decidedly unhappy. Oh dear thought Hobbys, I don't think she approves of a little dalliance on the side for married men.

Dr John Somerset, the king's secretary, detached himself from the surrounding nobles and officials to approach Hobbys.

'Ah William, thank you for coming, we have some work for you, some royal duties,' Somerset informed Hobbys, then added sotto voce, 'better than spending your days in the stews of Southwark eh?'

'The French are always supporting Scotland's border skirmishing. Now the King has secured an alliance with Burgundy, we are going to give the French a lesson. They seemed to have forgotten their place as subservient to the English monarchy in the sixty years since our great victory on St Crispin's day. The King is planning an invasion of France, you are to lead the medical team, you will be accompanied by two other Royal Physicians, William Hatteclyffe and Jacobus Fries, plus a dozen surgeons for the more menial roles. We will be leaving in two weeks, the King has his army nearly ready, so you will need to arrange all your equipment rapidly.'

Richard of Gloucester spotted him and summoned him to the front of the room. 'Good news for us all, we are going to give Louis XI a fair thrashing, should some excellent sport for our knights and archers, anything a Lancastrian King did at Agincourt, a Yorkist King can do better. There should be some fun for you Hobbys, you can do your post-mortem examinations on a few Frenchies, see if they are really gutless, eh Edward?'

Edward smiled at his brother, 'It is four years since we had such sport, we saw off the most ferocious Frenchie in Margaret of Anjou, Louis XI should be much easier. I need a little exercise, my courtiers keep me occupied here with papers, taxes and huge feasts, the only exercise I get is with….,' Edward tailed off as he looked at Jane Shore, then remembered his wife was also there, '….with some hunting when we can get to Windsor.'

Richard continued with enthusiasm, 'I want to lead a cavalry charge, that would be one of life's greatest pleasures, not the hard slog on foot like Barnet and Tewksbury, what do you say Edward?'

'I am sure that can be arranged for you, Anthony Rivers will be right alongside you.' replied Edward.

'And will you join us Ned, we can show those French curs something about English chivalry' Richard exclaimed passionately. 'If you won't charge with us, you can tell us the moment to go, nobody can read a battlefield like you Ned, you are the grandmaster of the chessboard battlefield, you must teach me, you never know when I will be leading my own army in your name.'

Elizabeth looking straight through him murmured, 'When you do lead a cavalry charge, my brother of Gloucester, it may not be to your liking.'

# FRANCE 1475

Slowly promised finance arrived with reluctance from the taxed populace, troops were gathered in Dover with ships to cross the channel and abundant supplies of weapons. Edward's army of some 11,000 men, including nearly all the nobility of England, landed in Calais, and set up preliminary camp free of any harassment from Louis. Edward and Richard continued to discuss their campaign and the pleasures of defeating the French on the battlefield.

Considerable numbers of French ladies arrived to provide services to the English soldiers. Edward commented that his army appeared welcome in France. After a week in Calais, Hobbys had discovered a local brothel, and was heading discretely back to his tent just before a misty dawn, ready to announce he had been on an urgent medical call if challenged. He skirted around the Royal Pavilion, when he saw a flap lift at the back, and a lady's head peep out, failing to notice Hobbys, she walked rapidly through the tent city to where a couple of riders were waiting for her under some trees with a spare horse, and they all rode away quietly. Very odd thought Hobbys, ladies of the night did not usually have escorts on horseback, though Edward was as likely to have found some upper class French courtesan as a local prostitute.

After a fortnight the army assembled in marching order, with the cavalry leading, resplendent with their armour and banners, scouts out on all sides, and the archers and foot soldiers following, and headed south-east. Rumours emerged from the royal pavilion that Edward seemed strangely less keen on battle than a few days before. After a month in France the French king sent couriers under a flag of truce to negotiate a peaceful settlement, letting it be known to Edward that he would prefer some treaty to open war fare. Louis proposed a meeting at Picquiny where a treaty could be drawn up and signed without spilling any blood. A combined tournament and other festivities were arranged, where the leading knights of each side could break a few capped lances, and hostilities were avoided, much to the disappointment of Gloucester who felt the agreement was without honour. He was disappointed to be deprived of a cavalry charge.

The two armies erected their pavilions half a mile apart, a central dais with thrones was erected and decked with the banners of the two kings and lavish coverings. The two kings approached the dais from opposite sides to fanfares from court musicians, climbed up and embraced in the middle, then sat on the richly carved thrones, followed by the Queen of France, Charlotte of Savoy, who sat on a smaller throne next to Louis.

Hobbys watched with mild interest, though was more impressed with the multitude of staggeringly beautiful ladies of the French court, wondering what joys the night may bring, when he was shocked on noticing the Queen, he had seen her before, he recognised her face, but from where? Then he recalled, she was the lady emerging from Edward's tent in Calais a few weeks ago! What could that mean? Had she been sent by Louis to negotiate a treaty, had she given Edward the one thing he craved for, had Louis been willing to sacrifice his own wife's fidelity knowing Edward's reputation, for the sake of his country, or more likely his exchequer?

It was rumoured among the French that she was none too beautiful, but skilled in the art of intimacy. And Louis had so many beautiful ladies around. No wonder Edward appeared to have suddenly changed his mind about fighting. Lucky Edward, he never appeared to have to pay for his many, many consorts, while Hobbys had to spend a large amount of his modest fees on women. Sometimes they made more than he did. Hobbys fancied the idea of being king for a day, or perhaps a night.

While negotiations were proceeding into the afternoon, Richard Chambry and John Staveley were looking over all the medical equipment, which it now seemed most likely to be unwanted, when they noticed Hobbys riding off the village past the forest. Wondering what would be taking the physician away from his duties at Picquiny, wondering if he had some other medical duties to perform, perhaps some free unostentatious treatment for a poor French peasant, and if he would need an assistant, after all Hobbys was the chief royal physician. Chambray followed Hobbys to the village where he rode straight to the hotel. He was not in the bar when Chambry followed, so he walked upstairs expecting Hobbys to be seeing a patient discreetly in a room there, and there in one of the rooms with the door open was a naked young lady in bed, and the service she was receiving from the king's physician was not of the medical kind, nor covered by the Hippocratic oath.

On his return Hobbys, somewhat distantly thinking of his recent delectable liaison, bumped into Gloucester, wandering disconsolately behind all the superficial ceremonies.

He greeted Hobbys with. 'Well Master William, you can put away your tools and bandages, our Lord, the King has negotiated a treaty with France, before my cavalry charge, or even a minor skirmish,' declared Richard, tossing his sword at the table in disgust, 'All those taxes, ships, knights, horses, archers and footmen for nothing. Henry V might have been a Lancastrian, but at least he had courage.'

Hobbys shared Gloucester's disappointment. Peace did not generate generous fees nearly as well as war, though he was somewhat relived that his sword remained sheathed again.

Gloucester wandered inconsonantly behind all the tents trying to curb his vexation, while in the central arena, French and English nobles wined and dined convivially having forgotten that they were about to fight a pitched battle a few days ago. The jousting with capped lances proceeded with much merriment and few hazards. He strolled along looking at his feet when he nearly bumped into Hobbys again. 'Master Hobbys, what are you doing, why are you not attending to the sick?' asked Richard.

'Your grace, 'replied Hobbys, 'may I present Dr Guillotine, the surgeon-generale of the French forces. We both feel our skills are unlikely to be required in the absence of serious combat, and were about to enjoy a common interest, a round or two with rapiers.'

'Master Guillotine and Master Hobbys, greetings. Such entertainment should be available for all to see. Such skill is undervalued by us brutes with battle-axes and broadswords. Pray bring your blades and demonstrate your skills before the kings.'

Hobbys and his French counterpart fought a 'first blood' encounter before the kings and their nobles to jeers of contempt for their feeble weapons with parry and thrust on lightening feet, before Hobbes finally drew first blood from his opponents arm.

'Excellent,' cheered Edward, 'my dear France and my brothers, was that not skilled?'

'Bah,' said George, 'Women's weapons wielded by cowards.'

'Well,' said Edward, 'my dear brother Clarence, why do you not try a few rounds with the royal physician, should you lose, he can repair the damage!'

'Brother king, a prince of the royal blood fight a mere physician with a woman's weapon? How undignified!' replied George.

'So you are afraid, one on one with an expert, dear Clarence,' taunted the king.

'Nonsense Ned,' replied Clarence, 'though I would rather an axe or a real sword, give me one of those toys and you will need to find yourself a new physician.'

"Your majesty, your grace,' called Hobbys, 'It is unfitting that I, a mere common physician should engage swords with a prince of the royal blood! Is this all just a jest?'

'No,' called Edward, Richard and George all together.

'Let us get on with this charade now!' said George.

'Your majesty, may we at least wear light helmets to protect our eyes, and capped rapiers in keeping with this joust?' asked Hobbys.

'Eye protection eh.' laughed Edward, 'A capital idea, young George there sometimes does not seem to see things clearly!' He guffawed at his own joke, slapping Gloucester on the arm, 'Yes give my Lord of Clarence a mask, but no caps on the rapiers, get to it.'

Hobbys and George saluted and circled, George, tall, elegant, handsome, attired in rich velvet, Hobbys, short, squat, attired in fustian, it looked an uneven contest. It was. George rushed at his opponent with vast air slashes, while Hobbys light footedly ducked and weaved, parried occasionally, easily evading George's impatient slashes. Edward and Richard laughed till tears ran down their cheeks.

'Enough!' called Edward, 'Hobbys, do not hesitate should a target present itself, just don't hurt poor George too much.'

'Brother King, you think he could blood me, you know little of my skills!' cried George.

Hobbys looked desperately at the King and Richard sitting nearby, only to be told to proceed.

After a couple of minutes circling in which Hobbys appeared discomforted, he engaged blades, then with a quick twist and flick, prised Georges sword out of his hand up into the air and held his blade to Georges neck. Clarence looked thunderously at Hobbys.

'One day, one night it will be men's swords, and the king will need a new physician,' he pouted, before storming off the field.

'Bravo,' cried Edward, 'so young Gloucester, do you wish to recover family honour? ''

'Only if ordered sire, only if you do not wish for the honour for yourself Ned.' responded Richard.

'Dickon, the honour is all yours brother, just to first blood,' conceded the king.

So they donned light helmets, bowed to Edward and saluted each other, searching for strengths and weaknesses in each other's eyes. There followed a memorable fight between two agile dextrous adversaries, they circled and jabbed, thrust and parried, locked swords and wrists, then thrust apart, neither able to gain an advantage for nigh on ten minutes, when Richard slipped under Hobbys guard and lightly grazed his arm. Hobbys dropped his sword, dropped on one knee, and gasped, 'your grace is a great swordsman, I am your man in life and limb and earthly worship,' while the crowds roared in approval. It was the nearest to a conflict they would see on this field.

# ST PAULS CATHEDRAL – THE CHURCH COURT 1476

Hobbys responded to the summons to attend the public court of St Paul's cathedral. Alice had warned him that this would happen shortly and that he should answer for his sins. Entering into the court, he saw Alice sitting close to the front facing the dais.

Shortly the clerk called, 'All rise.' The dean and deacon of the cathedral entered looking grave and appearing resplendent in their robes. They nodded to the clerk, sat down and looked at their agenda for the day. A clerk sat just below them, with a pile of blank paper, an inkwell and many quills.

The clerk called out, 'the first case before us today, your honours is the case of Alice Hobbys against her husband William Hobbys.' The dean surveyed Alice with a reassuring smile, frowned at William, and asked Alice, 'Could you outline the nature of your case against your husband for the court.'

Alice wiped away a few tears and commenced falteringly, 'your grace, I have been married to my husband William for twenty years, and we have five children. I have always been a good and faithful wife. I was therefore deeply shocked three months ago, when my neighbour said there was a rumour in the street that my husband had been seen not just once, but on many occasions in the brothels of this city. I confronted him with this knowledge, and demanded to know how long this had been going on. Slowly, reluctantly, he admitted to serial infidelity starting in 1462, when we had only been married six years with many women in the city of London and Southwark, and then in brothels in Calais, Saint-Omer and Peronne, Picardy in France during the King's campaign there and on many occasions, so many he cannot remember the names of any of them. I suspect this infidelity may have even started earlier when he was at university.'

The dean clucked sympathetically, 'Awful my dear, please sit down and compose yourself, clerk of the court, are there any witnesses to these events?'

'Yes your worship,' 'responded the clerk, 'We actually have four of the defendant's medical colleagues to testify, all upright citizens of great integrity.'

Hobbys felt relieved, his colleagues would testify to his excellent standing in the medical profession, to his clinical excellence, and his position in the highest house in the land, this ordeal may not be as bad as he had first feared.

The Dean enquired to the Clerk, 'For whom do these gentlemen appear?' The Clerk smirked at Hobbys, 'Why for Mrs Hobbys of course.' Hobbys was dumbfounded. 'Mm," said the Dean, most unusual, these doctors usually stick together when confronted with the law, call the first witness.'

'Surgeon Richard Chambyr,' summoned the clerk. After taking the oath, Chambyr related that he was one of the surgeons accompanying Edward's French campaign, and that he saw Hobbys naked in a bed with an equally naked prostitute in a brothel in Peronne, and that he told Hobbys he was surprised and disappointed by such behaviour which ill-befitted a married man or a medical man.

'Thank you surgeon Chambyr,' said the dean, "master Hobbys, do you wish to cross examine this witness?'

'No, er no no no thank you your Honour,' Hobbys stammered.

'Surgeon John Stavely,' summoned the clerk. Hobbys hoped with good reason that his apprentice and son-in-law would be on his side, however, having taken the oath, Stavely confirmed this sighting in the French brothel in Peronne, and then added that he had also seen Hobbys in brothels in Calais and Saint-Omer as well. Stavely's testament reminded him of his visit to 'la Boudoir du Domination' in Saint-Omer, and the unique experiences he gained there, wow, that had been stimulating, frightening, exciting. Hobbys wrists and ankles tingled at the memory of the bonds that had rendered him deliciously, frighteningly helpless, what a naughty pair Francoise and Jacqueline had been.

'Master Hobbys, this is a serious case, are you listening to the proceedings and paying attention?'

Hobbys became aware that the Dean was addressing him and the court was awaiting an answer. Again, hoping that was what he had been asked, he declined to cross examine. Stavely followed Chambyr out of the witness box.

'Summon Thomas Rolf,' called the Clerk. Hobbys had hoped that his fellow Barber-Surgeons may have something good to say about him, but now he feared the worst.

Thomas Rolf and Robert Haliday both recalled an incident when they had been summoned to a brothel in Southward to treat the brothel keeper, and while there were shocked to see Hobbys and a young lady, a very young lady, naked in bed together. Both expressed disappointment and Haliday said to the Court, 'I informed the guild of barber surgeons who then reprimanded Hobbys for unprofessional behaviour.'

'Thank you gentlemen, master William Hobbys, how do you plead?' said the dean.

Hobbys came to his feet, 'your Worship, I do not believe I am being tried for a crime, and that I do not need to plead guilty or not guilty. I acknowledge these misdemeanours and regret any embarrassment to my profession, which I have always served to the best of my ability, and have excellent references from the highest in the land. Many do not see my activities as unusual, and many from high offices in the land have also been seen in Southwark' Hobbys stated, trying to limit the damage to his reputation and practice. He wondered how the king had always got away with similar activities and never had to answer to a court.

Hobbys continued, 'Your honours, may I state that not long ago in the time of King Richard II, the Southwark stews were owned by the bishop of Winchester, and rented out by William Walworth, the mayor of London. Presumably the church did not disapprove of such establishments then, and there was no law stating that married men were obliged to be faithful.' A titter of laughter ran around the court.

The dean and deacon frowned, and the deacon continued, 'The bishop was anointed in God's holy orders, be careful who you blaspheme, Master Hobbys. May I inform you that the saintly Bishop of Westminster in all his holy innocence, was apparently not aware of the difference between a bawdy house and a boarding house. He believed his property was providing a safe refuge for the homeless young women of South London, a sanctuary for their virginity. It is reported that he was somewhat surprised by the rather large rental money blessing his church coffers.'

'SILENCE!' The dean shouted banging on the desk with his gavel, as raucous laughter echoed around the old court building, 'Do you have anything else to say in your defence, Master Hobbys?'

'I must inform the court that my wife Alice, has often been unwelcoming when I have been obliged to work long hours, at times I have felt unwanted in my own house and my own bed, I regret that I succumbed like many men to seeking a little comfort elsewhere at times, particularly when campaigning with the king's army in France, when I never knew if this day may be my last. Also your worship knows I was present at the battles of Barnet and Tewksbury, and men commonly seek relief both before and after the stress of such events. My wife Alice has rejected my attempts at apologising and restoring our relationship in the last few months, she has contemptuously refused all my attempts at repairing our relationship and re-establishing some intimacy. Your honour I am but a poor hard working barber-surgeon who has been subject to many stresses in life and I beg you to look on my minor misdemeanours with understanding and forgiveness.'

The Dean and Deacon looked bored and unimpressed by this monologue and whispered together briefly, before the dean announced, 'Alice Hobbys, we find that you have been treated badly by your husband. We have heard from Richard Chambry and John Stavely, then Thomas Rolf and Robert Haliday of your husband's adultery on at many occasions in many places. We agree with the guild of barber-surgeons that this behaviour is quite unbecoming for an eminent doctor. We appreciate this was a terrible shock to you. We consider this behaviour a serious breach of canon law and unbecoming for the king's physician. We grant you the right to quit your husband's bed and board as a legally separated woman, and to claim a quarter of his property and assets.'

The dean symbolically picked up a ribbon and cut it into two pieces, indicating the hand fasting ceremony of marriage, the binding of the bride and groom's hand with ribbons, was now formally terminated. Hobbys registered surprise, if having a mistress was grounds for a separation, there wouldn't be a married couple left in Westminster Palace, now Henry VI had gone straight to heaven.

The crowded court was immediately struck dumb, then full of surprised whispers between the predominantly male observers. They had not expected that men's visits to a brothel would result in a court verdict of adultery against any man, and indeed that such visits actually were considered adultery. Everyone knew there were three sorts of intercourse, one with your own wife, nice but dull, one with another man's wife if you were lucky, nice and very naughty, though that was adultery, and then sex with a prostitute which didn't really count as adultery. One of the women present incensed by such comments shouted to Hobbys, 'Serves you right you dirty bastard!' as Hobbys vacated the court pursued by the Clerk seeking the quarter of his assets.

# THE TOWER FEBRUARY 19TH 1478

The corpulent body lay on Hobbys slab. George, the first Duke of Clarence lay under the eagle eye of William Hobbys, pale, naked and very dead. The king had finally realised he could not trust one who had broken faith, not once but many times, even if it were his brother, especially because it was his brother. As George was a convicted felon, the king had allowed Hobbys to examine the body.

Hobbys reflected with sadness, that opposing thoughts and irreconcilable opinions could generate a stimulating debate among friends, but either sullen avoidance or overt warfare among close family members. George never thought about the consequences of his actions beyond his own personal gains, it reminded Hobbys of a Cambridge tutor quoting Socrates, *the unexamined life is not worth living.* Well, Hobbys was about to remedy that deficiency in the duke's life, he would examine George in greater detail than George ever examined himself.

His pale skin had a yellowy tinge; peering at the sclera Hobbys noted the same colour. George had been enjoying an excess of malmsey long before being drowned in it. Hobbys wondered if the soldiers of the tower were enjoying the full butt of malmsey surprisingly donated to them this morning, or indeed if they were aware of its previous use, or what other body fluids might have been added overnight.

Continuing his inspection of the body, Hobbys noted other tell-tale signs of liver disease, even in death the palms were red, the contracture of the hands was in Hobbes opinion a sign of excess ale and wine, he must describe that next professional meeting to his colleagues. Hopefully in the near future he would obtain the royal charter to found a College of Physicians. There were red spots over the skin as described by Avicenna as a sign of excess drinking. There was a dark mark under the left nipple, Hobbys moved the candle closer. There were some tattooed letters, partially erased, it said............

'Oh God!' exclaimed the doctor. It said *King George 1ˢᵗ 1471*. Hobbys would not be telling Edward IV that finding.

Hobbys picked up his scalpel, and sliced carefully and firmly down the midline from the breastbone to the pubic bone into the abdomen releasing large quantities of yellow fluid that ran over George's flanks, flooded the slab, and fell onto the stone floor before disappearing down the drain in the floor. Hobbys reflected that Elizabeth Wydville, Edward's queen would have enjoyed doing that some years ago. The internal examination revealed a hard large nodular liver, an even larger spleen, both lungs congested with sour smelling wine and some hard white deposits, maybe an excess of calcium, on the small shrunken pancreas, perhaps that was also a new finding caused by wine he could describe to his colleagues. He hoped they would be impressed by his skills. Second to the handsome fees he obtained as the royal physician, he loved the esteem and approbation of other physicians, though obviously with overt modesty.

After looking around the abdomen and finding no other abnormality, Hobbys sutured the two sides of the abdominal wall together and covered the body with the Yorkist flag left in the room. Finally, in death he was at one with his brothers!

Hobbys thought he could become as eminent as John Argentine who was considered the cleverest physician around even though he was seventeen years younger than Hobbys, and lacked Hobbys experience and practical skills. Going to Eton, then going to King's College, Cambridge, followed by studying medicine in Padua, where he claimed to have graduated with an MD, and Ferrara till a couple of years ago had certainly given him a lot of knowledge, though to Argentine's credit he was more than willing to share his and other's ideas. His recipes, always done in Latin to impress his readers with his erudition, included a novel form of therapy for sciatica used by a lady on a friar in Herefordshire a couple of years ago, and another new therapy used by his friend, Master William Ordew, on a Cambridgeshire Rector with hectic fever. Hobbys wondered if the vocation of these two patients had assisted in their recovery.

Argentine has taken to inscribing his books 'zouan Agentein' in the Venetian style, an affectation that appeared to impress other people thought Hobbys. The King had made Argentine physician to his seven-year-old son, an appointment that still disappointed Hobbys, especially as Argentine was nowhere to be seen when fighting may need to be done as when Hobbys accompanied the king to France.

# FETTER LANE, JANUARY 1479

Two messengers arrived almost simultaneously as Hobbys busied himself with the day's practice, a couple of wealthy merchants had swelled his coffers for the day, improving Hobbys mood and self-esteem. The first messenger informed Hobbys that there was a new epidemic in South London, with a dozen or more people sick with high fever, spots and black lumps in the groin. Hobbys could recognise the plague. There was nothing to benefit doctors to treat such unfortunate sufferers, they all died, which would not enhance a doctor's reputation, none paid their bills, and most important, the poor doctor could succumb to the disease, as some of his colleagues did last time the disease appeared in London. No, a trip to see some of his wealthy patients living outside London be good for his health, pocket and reputation as a compassionate physician.

The second messenger wore the regalia of the king. 'You master Hobbys, the king's physician?' he inquired. Hobbys nodded acquiescence. 'His majesty wants you in the palace now, with your equipment.'

Hobbys grabbed his medical bag full of his latest medications and surgical instruments, always ready at the door for a royal summons, ordered the stable boy to saddle his horse and placed the sign, 'Gone to Westminster Palace' on the door. That he knew impressed the local population, and attracted the wealthier local businessmen and their families.

# WESTMINSTER PALACE

Hobbys sank on one knee before the king and queen. 'Ah Master Hobbys,' said Elizabeth, 'You will have heard the plague has returned to London, we will be moving to Etham where God's grace will protect us from pestilence. My Lord Stanley will be moving to Windsor Castle, with our beloved youngest son, George, Duke of Bedford. You will accompany Stanley and be responsible for the health of the royal party, and especially our beautiful son. We believe he will be safest in your most expert care.' She looked at him threateningly, 'do not let us down Master Hobbys!'

'Your majesty, I am pleased that you should follow the recommendation of my illustrious predecessor, Guy de Chauraic, a survivor of the plague. He said "go quickly, go far, and return slowly" I am also deeply honoured that you entrust the Duke to my care, I shall protect him with my life.'

# WINDSOR CASTLE, FEBRUARY 1479

Hobbys entered the Great Hall of the Upper Ward of Windsor Castle recalling his unpleasant and humiliating appearance in the court of St Pauls, as the massive royal castle had been constructed mainly in the time of Edward III, under the supervision of the 'saintly' William of Wykeham, then the owner of Southwark stews. He had requested an audience with Stanley, a difficult man always on the lookout for his own advantage, an arrogant man who appeared not to understand the importance of Hobbys role.

Hobbys bowed briefly, Lord Stanley would not be having his knee. 'My Lord, as you are aware, King Edward placed me in charge of all health issues in this castle. I have observed that men from outside are entering the castle to bring in supplies, and roaming around near the royal apartments. I have seen the young prince being carried in the gardens by his nurse past such men. It was my command that all supplies should be left at the gate, and that the king's servants inside the castle should collect these supplies.'

Stanley, appearing astonished, raised his hand, 'Silence knave.' he started.

Hobbys continued, 'I require that you order all bearers of supplies to the castle to deposit their wares at the front gate and withdraw before the castle staff bring such supplies into the castle, and to…' Stanley raised a hand, 'Cease knave, do you know who I am, a descendant of kings, from the family of Edward III, how dare you think you can speak to me like this, you clearly did not hear our lord, King Edward put me in charge of this castle.'

Hobbys undaunted replied, 'the king put you in charge of managing the castle, but he ordered me to care for the health of all here, and especially the Duke of Bedford, he acknowledges that I am the expert in this area, and that my opinion should have precedence over anyone who is not an expert. You will answer to the king should little Prince George suffer any disease if your management blocks professional expertise.'

Stanley, incandescent with rage and surprise, believing that his paramount status far exceeded any menial knowledge, drew his sword and shouted to his guards, 'throw this varlet out and into the cess pit.' Hobbys was manhandled in an undignified fashion out of the great hall, but just short of the cess pit, he informed the guards they may catch plague if they approached too close to the cesspit. Daunted by this prospect, they looked around for a large muddy puddle and threw Hobbys into that.

Hobbys, equally furious, arose, his dignity covered in mud, shouted over his shoulder, 'You, my Lord Stanley, have been observed not using the aquamanile to wash your hands before and after the banquets.' He then withdrew to his chambers to improve his appearance and temper.

Two weeks later, he was summoned to little George's royal apartment to find the toddler lying inert in bed, breathing heavily, with red blotches on his legs and fiery hot skin. He clearly had caught the plague as Hobbys had feared. 'All staff out except for his nurse maid,' Hobbys ordered, 'You and I will wear face masks, spoon a mixture of honey, water and if you have any, powdered marigold flowers into his mouth every hour. I have a plague votive of St Roch, who's prayers were answered by God when he caught the plague, to place around little George's neck. Fill this aquamanile lion with water at the top, and run it over your hands before and after every time you tough the prince. We must send a message to the king about his son being seriously ill. So where is spawn of Edward ill now, the man who thought his importance was greater than my knowledge now?'

'Master Hobbys' responded one of George's guards, 'if you refer to my Lord Stanley, he left over an hour ago when he heard the Duke was unwell, stating that you were responsible for all health matters, and I believe he has retired to Castle Donnington. He asked me also to tell you that he had a moral duty to ensure the health of one of the king's important advisers, himself!'

Sadly, inevitably, little Prince George deteriorated and died the following day.

# WESTMINSTER PALACE APRIL 1479

Edward lounged back on the couch, Jane Shaw beside him. 'Leave us sweetness for a moment; I will see you later tonight.' he said to Jane. 'Ah Hobbys, we thank you for your attention to our poor little son, Stanley assures us that neither you nor he could have done any more for my poor little George.' Hobbys jaw dropped, realizing that the secretary who 'took' his letter was a Stanley man. Edward continued, 'the position of master of St Mary of Bethlehem has become vacant, it is a hospital for the insane with a generous stipend. It is yours in return for your faithful service for so many years, perhaps you could arrange for Margaret Beaufort to be admitted there, and stop her complaining that her son should have a greater status here, in spite of his various bastard bloodlines.'

'Your majesty, Lord Stanley considered he should firstly ensure the safety of his person because of his importance of the royal council, hence he left for Castle Dennington at the first sign of plague.' Edward looked a little surprised and thoughtful.

Hobbys continued, 'as always you are too generous to your humble physician especially as this position has always been held by a man of God. However, I believe I can bring my experience to the unfortunate inmates with benefit, thank you again sire." Hobbys mentally added the new stipend to his current assets.

Seeing an advantage with the king looking relaxed and contented, Hobbys thought he could give a little medical advice man to man.

The king was usually a friendly affable man to whom one could speak frankly, though he could go into towering rages when crossed. Edward was perceived as being notoriously promiscuous. He still seduced women successfully, randomly, married or single, noble or peasant, none seemed to refuse him, yet after conquest he discarded them to his friends to seek new challenges. He also consumed nearly as much ale and wine as poor old George. Hobbys thought he would take a risk and continued.

'Almighty Sovereign, I am your most humble servant in all things, you can order my detention, exile or execution,' said Hobbys on his knees, 'But you have appointed me as your royal physician, so I will have my say. You were a mighty prince, the greatest warrior in Christendom, you fought and won seven battles, but you have been led astray, you have been misguided by the most beautiful Jane Shore, and led into corruption by your brother-in-law Dorset, who incidentally beds Mistress Jane when you are not looking. You have lost your robust good health, your manly physique, even your manhood. The Queen has been without child for a few years.'

'Have you finished yet?' growled Edward. 'bloody doctors and hospitals are a problem, We gave the Master of St Leonard's Hospital in York the right to raise the peppercorn tax from local farmers in the Chancery Court last year, and this has apparently started some uprising in the north. John Neville, the Earl of Northumberland, will sort them out for us. Have you finished Hobbys?'

'No sire, your stature in all ways is too great, you have become too large, two or three men can no longer lift you, you piss a lot and the urine you passed just now tastes sweet. By the writings of our guide and mentor, the great Avicenna I think you have diabetes. One of my great predecessors in medicine, Gilbertus Anglicus wrote a book over 200 years ago, the Compendium Medicinae in which he describes the problem, and considers that it is caused by much meddling with women and drinking strong wine. I beg you, your Majesty to heed my words and be a little more circumspect with women and wine.

Diabetes can cause early death, yet your dearly beloved son is still a minor, while greedy barons circle round the child. He needs you to guide him to manhood before he is ready to take the throne. I beg you again to return to the training yard, and moderate your consumption of wine, food and women.'

'Begone' roared Edward, 'you are a bigger pain in the arse than all my priests put together, is a man to have no pleasures in life?'

Hobbys backed out hastily.

An hour later Hobbys sat at his desk struggling with the Arabic in Avicenna's text *'The Cannon of Medicine'*; he needed to remind himself of the master's treatment of diabetes. The ancient Egyptian physician Hesy-Ra had described the problem of passing large quantities of urine, known as polyuria three and a half millennia ago in the Ebers papyrus, a copy of which was in the Oxford Bodleian Library. The Greek physician Aretaeus of Cappadocia in 250 B.C. was the first to call this Diabetes, and about this time physicians in India had noticed that ants were attracted to sweet urine. Nearly 500 years ago, the great Persian physician, Avicenna has described an abnormal appetite leading to sweet urine and problems in achieving an erection. Sadly Hobbys though most of his were wasted these days.

There was a gentle knock on his door. 'Come in,' he called, and, to his amazement, in walked Jane Shore. 'Mistress Jane, it is my pleasure to see you, I trust your visit is not due to any ill health. I hope you are allowing our sovereign lord some rest,' he rose from his chair as she walked around his desk to stand beside him, looking briefly into his eyes.

'I am well thanking you Master William,' she paused, looking down at his feet. 'We all know how much you love the king, and how much you worry about his health, you are right, he is not as robust as a few years ago.' She paused again, then lifted her eyes to look directly into his through her pale eyelashes. 'Edward feels you do not understand his needs as a man,' and with that she kissed him lightly on the lips, when he did not respond or withdraw, she kissed him again, long and firm. She felt him return her pressure. Reaching up to her shoulders she pulled two bows loose and her gown fell to the floor at Hobbys feet. She was naked in front of him, beautiful, available, experienced, and skilful. Hobbys trembled; he had not been intimate with Alice for some years even before their separation owing to the damage she suffered with the birth of their last child. She had said she would understand if he needed another woman. Sarah and Carole were pleasant but distant memories, and the few recent dalliances in Southwark had not measured up to the skills of the ladies of France.

Jane took his hands in hers and walking backwards drew him towards his inner chamber. Hobbys thought he had not had a woman in Westminster Palace, certainly not one of the king's ladies, there was always a risk of a forbidden intimate relationship with one of his patients. However, Jane had never seen him as a patient, and although she was married, he wasn't, so he would not really be committing adultery. Also it appeared to him that the palace priests were experienced and forgiving in the confessional box with this sin. Hobbys conscience dissolved and he followed her into his bed chamber, wondering idly what became of Sarah in Oxford, and if Dorset was allowed to bed Jane, then perhaps he would not be executed should Jane tell Edward, it sounded as if he encouraged this visit.

# FETTER LANE 1481

Jacob returned for more balsam having a recurrence of his rather personal health problem. 'Master Hobbys,' he said, 'I think you will be packing your wagon and heading north very soon, this time for the king's loyal brother warrior, Gloucester. King Edward's treaty with Scotland as you know terminated last year following the Scots raid on Bamburgh Castle led by the Duke of Angus, and reprisal attacks on Scotland led by the Earl of Northumberland. Edward's spies have reported the arrival of French ships in Leith bearing artillery and expert gunners, the 'auld alliance' has become active again. Edward has set up a naval blockade of the Firth of Forth and attacked Blackness Castle. He sent messages northward complaining of the Scottish occupation of Berwick, Roxburgh and Coldringham, and of the Scots failure to pay homage to Edward, sped. King James is strengthening the walls of Berwick, though the pope is calling for peace between the two countries. Master Hobbys, war is always a good time to buy gold, but we also expect a blockade of French wine, and we have some bottles worth buying before they become possibly rare and expensive, or more likely, unavailable.'

# SCOTLAND 1481 BATTLE CAMP

Richard strode into his marquee, brushing mud and dust from his tunic. Northumberland, Catesby, Lovell and Ratcliffe followed, all attended by a retinue of pages. Richard removed his helmet and gloves and glowered around him. 'So, do you think James will commit his army to a battle, we are here on his soil outnumbered by his army, why does the man hesitate to provide us with some sport?' Lovell passed Richard a goblet of wine, and a hot chicken leg from the chafing dish, and opinioned, 'James has heard of your prowess on the battlefield, his control over his nobles is weak, they may desert him, or even turn on him and crown his brother.'

A broad man entered and knelt before Richard. "Your grace, I am William Hobbys, physician to His Majesty, King Edward. He bids me to say that court matters prevent him joining you on this campaign, but he wishes you success in subduing these wild Celts and offers my services to tend to you and your army should hostilities generate employment for me.'

'Thank you Master Hobbys, arise. I remember you well, you did your best for my dear late father and brother before Wakefield. You kindly sewed my arm together after the battle of Barnet. I well remember your joust with my unfortunate brother George during our failed campaign in France, it was indeed one of the funniest things I ever saw. I am disappointed that my brother the king will not be able to join our sport, how is our noble sovereign?" Hobbys hesitated then replied, 'his majesty is excellently well, your grace,' The pause was not lost on Richard.

Richard and his nobles aided by their knights of the body removed their armour and refiled their wine goblets, the king having generously provided eighty butts of wine for the campaign, as he was unable to come himself. Pages removed their armour for cleaning and polishing for campaigning on the morrow. In the absence of any opposition Richard intended to enter Edinburgh, and occupy the Royal Scottish Palace of Holyrood.

Richard striped of his shirt, turned away and bent over the bowl of water to wash his face and hands before the banquet. Hobbys gasped in dismay.

'Your grace, your grace, oh no, you are unwell, your back, oh my lady, are you in pain?'

'What do you mean Master Hobbys, you look as if you have seen a ghost,' a bemused Richard responded.

'Your Grace, may I speak to you in private confidence as your physician.' Richard waved his hand cursorily, dismissing Catesby and the other knights of his body, but indicating to Lovell that he should remain.

'So what ails you man, am I not the picture of health, maybe not as big and strong as my brother in his prime as a warrior king?' inquired Gloucester.

'Your grace, I er I er you..,' stammered Hobbys, 'you have a curvature of your spine, known by the ancient Greek physicians as a scoliosis. Has anyone noted this before? Do you suffer from discomfort or pain in your back, do you ever feel short of breath? Allow me to give you some agrimony and mugwort, the leaves and roots in old swine grease and vinegar are a proven remedy for back ache.'

'What rubbish do you speak, I am the second Knight of the Kingdom,' said Richard scornfully, 'Francis, do you have any idea what he is talking about?'

Francis looked embarrassed, an awkward silence followed as Richard looked at him quizzically.

'Dickon, my lord, we er I have noted some er irregularity of your back, but we did not want to say anything about it. You have said your back is sometimes sore after a day in the saddle but it did not seem to bother you too much.'

'Your Grace, do hold this mirror in front of you while I hold this one behind you and look at the line of your spine when you are bending over,' pleaded Hobbys.

Richard peered at the mirror and gasped in horror. 'God's blood, Hobbys what does this mean?'

'Your Grace, if you have little pain and no shortness of breath, it may means little, but I must insist on providing for you the best available treatment.'

'And what would that be, I remember my brother saying he did not like some of your advice. He said he had found a way of ensuring your silence, what was that Master Hobbys?'

'Your Grace, I have no idea what he could have meant' mumbled Hobbys hoping Richard had no idea, 'the treatment is very simple, will only take a few hours per day, and not be too costly.'

'A few hours! explain in more detail,' growled Richard.

'Your Grace, these methods were first proposed by the father of medicine, Hippocrates, he saw the spine as the keel of the body, a foundation stone for life itself. His ideas were endorsed by the great Persian physician, Avicenna. You should have a hot bath, then lie face down on a board. I will tie cloth bands under your arm pits, and others around your legs and hips. We will then pull them in opposite directions, while placing some royal paste and pressure on your spine,' pleaded Hobbys. 'The royal paste, I will request John Clerk, the king's apothecary who has come with me, to blend it for you. It is a mixture of sugar, honey, ginger, mace, cloves and theriac, available for only a modest fee. The whole treatment will straighten out your spine before anyone other than the three of us in this room becomes aware that you have a health problem.

Richard scowled. 'What a load of rubbish, you want to stretch me, it sounds like the rack!'

Hobbys wheedled, 'Your Grace, the traction is applied gently at first according to tolerance, if you prefer, we can tie you upside-down on a ladder.'

Richard thundered, 'I can get this done on the rack in the tower for free without having to pay extortionate medical fees. I don't have time for hours of treatment daily, think of something more suitable.'

'Well you Grace, we can put on a brace to prevent your spine bending further,' begged Hobbys.

'You mean a brace like a suit of armour?' asked Richard.

'Yes your grace, like a suit of armour,' answered Hobbys.

'Fine,' said Richard, 'the matter is settled, I shall wear my suit of armour daily for my campaign against the Scots, and that will keep us all happy. Our saviour endured much more pain than I feel, any discomfort I bear will remind me of his suffering. A life without any pain diminishes life's achievements. Be gone, Master Hobbys, with all your unpleasant ideas, how did my brother persuade you not to nag all the time, you are worse than a man's wife and priest combined.'

Hobbys reflected that another liaison with Jane Shore would leave him speechless, but he was not going to mention that. Richard totally disapproved of the loose morals in Edward's court.

He had one last try, 'your grace, should you have pain or shortness of breath at a later date, which you may have, I would be pleased to help, perhaps for a little discount, it is an honour to serve you great family.'

'Go!' shouted Lovell and Richard together.

Hobbys stepped out of the tent and was immediately assaulted by the freezing driving rain so common in Scotland. He inadvertently looked over his shoulder as many did in the godforsaken country will an illogical fear of things felt but not seen. It was as though the long-dead spirits of Scotland had awoken in anger at the presence of an English army on their soil, and were hell-bent on seeking revenge. There was an aura to this country, a magic in the soil that usually inspired their wild Celtic warriors to feats of superhuman bravery in spite of overwhelming odds. Neither Richard not his followers could understand why the Scots held back when they had superior numbers a few leagues away.

# FOTHERINGHAY CASTLE JUNE 1482

The King sat in front of a roaring fire. 'God's blood Dickon, it is so cold up here, even in summer. I'm sorry I cannot accompany you to subdue those blue-arsed barbarians north of the border, but problems in the palace demand my attention. Hastings and Dorset are at each other's throats if I am not there to keep the peace, and Dorset crawls into Jane's bed, she seems unable to last a few days without a man. Gods-blood, she is so lusty, she totally wears me out, she really is the merriest harlot in England, but I don't seem to satisfy her as well as previous years.'

Richard endeavoured to keep his expression neutral and not show the disapproval he felt. A king should behave with some decorum, at least on the surface.

Edward announced that he had a meeting with Alexander, the Duke of Albany and brother of James III of Scotland, after Alexander had landed at Southampton. The English would support his attempt to wrest the throne from his brother in return for homage being paid to Edward and Berwick upon Tweed being seceded to England. Edward continued, 'John Elrington here will be your war treasurer, Francis Lovell is on the way to be your second-in-command. John, inform my lord of Gloucester of what you have organised.'

'My lord' said Elrington, 'The king has assembled an army of twenty-thousand men to attack Scotland by land and sea. You will have two thousand sheaves of arrows and over a hundred horses to draw your ordinance.'

Edward resumed, 'I hope James will finally show some courage and provide some sport for your army, you don't need me there, and you have won your spurs many times over. I can however provide you again with the best physician in our court. Master Hobbys will come with you again, clerk, read the terms for me.'

Edward's clerk read form a document, 'the king has already arranged with the roll of accounts to pay Master Hobbys two shillings a day, plus eight surgeons on one shilling, and our apothecary John Clerk, who was paid in total £13 16s 9½d for his services and divers medicines.'

Edward continued, 'Dickon, I think you should take first besiege and take Berwick back from the perfidious Scots, so it becomes part of our kingdom from henceforth, then take Edinburgh and quarter in Holyrood palace.'

Hobbys had accompanied Edward to Fotheringhay, and would depart for Scotland with Gloucester. He had sat quietly listening to Edward's terms. It was an excellent position, he enjoyed working in a medical team when he led the team, there would be an esprit de corps that recognised his eminence. Gloucester and Albany recaptured the town of Berwick and proceeded to Edinburgh. Hobbys had only a limited number of battle casualties to treat, injured Scots were deemed by the English as not worthy of expert surgical attention. As the previous year, James avoided a pitched battle, Richard quartered his army in Holyrood House, but lacked the ordinance to besiege Edinburgh Castle, where James resided trying to control the different factions of Scottish power and nobility. A truce was negotiated and signed on August 4th 1482, and the English army returned south to capture Berwick Castle before the end of August before Richard went to Middleham, Hobbys back to Westminster, and Albany to a position of shared power in Scotland.

# FETTER LANE OCTOBER 1482

Hobbys and Jacob shared their observations of events of the last year. Jacob said, 'the king is no longer the great warrior of yesteryear, indeed the queen worries for his health. Young Prince Edward is not old enough for the throne yet. Clearly Gloucester is first knight of this kingdom now, a potentially unstable situation.' Hobbys and Jacob peered into the fire, trying to decipher the future in the flames.

# WESTMINSTER PALACE MARCH 28TH 1483

The morning was fine and bright, spring was in the air. 'We shall have some sport today,' cried Edward looking out of the window, 'let us take a boat out on the Thames at Chelsea and go fishing. God will approve of us fishing on Good Friday once we have attended mass. Sadly Hobbys reflected this was Edward's favourite activity, now that his bulk prevented all the more vigorous pursuits of his youth. 'We won't need you Master Hobbys, as we all feel well and you will only try to stop us having fun.'

Edward's fun these days was too much wine and too much food, though his days of wenching were rare. The queen watched concerned, unsure if she preferred him fit and unfaithful, or unhealthy with little libido.

Hobbys also looked on with concern. Edward had not been himself since Louis XI of France had rejected the previous betrothal of Edward's daughter Elizabeth to the Dauphin in favour of Margaret, the daughter of Maximilian of Austria and Duke of Burgundy. Even the pension received from Louis, a corner stone of Edward's financial policy ceased. Edward appeared depressed and withdrew into increasing quantities of wine. There was also a rumour in court that Lord Rivers had asked Andrew Dymock, his London lawyer, for a copy of his letters patent appointing him as Governor of the Prince of Wales, with the power to move the prince or raise troops in case anything happened to Edward, and Rivers needed to act to maintain the Wydville control over the nation. Hobbys wondered if the Queen was aware of problems with the King's health.

Hobbys concern increased when he looked out the window at lunch time as a distant rumble caught his attention to see a sudden change in the weather. The sun had disappeared behind dark clouds and fog was rolling up the river. He ran down to the courtyard, grabbed one of the horses kept saddled for emergencies and galloped down the river to Chelsea.

While on horseback he recalled as he hastened out, he had glimpsed Margaret Beaufort coming in furtively clutching a bunch of foxgloves. He had seen Margaret a few times at gatherings in the great hall in Westminster, though they had never communicated or been introduced, she had never sought his medical assistance, preferring her own physician. She always appeared deep in thought, lost in her own private world. Her secret plots remained hidden under a veneer of polite smiles and proclaimed religious superiority, while her professed concern for the members of the Yorkist court always seemed false. Her unblinking gaze went straight through everyone in a disconcerting fashion. You would no more turn your back on her than you would on a viper. Strangely she saw herself as the equal to Edward and Elizabeth, nay even their superior, yet her grandfather was conceived in the adulterous relationship between John of Gaunt, himself possibly not the child on Edward III, and Katherine Swynford, when both were married to others. Richard II had legitimised their relationship, though few accepted that law, once a bastard, always a bastard most thought. Even Richard declared the family barred from the throne.

Margaret also had a lofty opinion of the importance of her only son, Henry Tudor, now an outcast hiding in France. Yet that Tudor also had dubious parentage on the male side, his grandfather, Owen Tudor, a Welsh nobody had apparently seduced and possibly married the widowed queen of Henry V, Catherine of Valois without royal approval, and possibly when she was already pregnant from a liaison with Edmund Beaufort, the second Duke of Somerset. Hobbys thought his background was superior to that collection of illegitimate opportunists. While he scarcely registered sighting her at the time, the odder he thought this was. Margaret had always preferred red roses to any other flower. Foxgloves could be poisonous and needed careful handling and disposal. Margaret never did anything without careful planning, she was up to something, Hobbys would try to keep an eye on her.

A few miles along the river, Hobbys found the royal barge, partially visible in the fog, bottles of wine slung over the side to keep them cool, and more sitting empty in the boat along with a few fish. The elegant party of young men and women were looking anxiously at the sky and the king as the first few heavy drops of rain landed in the uncovered boat.

Hobbys looked at the king in dismay. 'Sire, your majesty, fishing in this weather with your state of health would be the greatest folly. The fog is thick and very cold, and you are coughing and coughing. You should get back to the palace and remain in bed where I can minister to you.'

Once back in the palace having dried off and changed, Edward appeared back to his hearty self, he indulged in a lot of wine for supper, and meat, salad, oranges and other fruits, a bad combination of heating and cooling food for a man with a sensitive digestion. Philippe de Commynes, when he was French Ambassador to Edward's court always commented that too much fruit and vegetables would cause apoplexy. Edward had obtained a dispensation from the Pope several years ago to omit fish at Lent and on Holy Days as this had caused vomiting and diarrhoea, though I had wondered if this was due to mixing too much red wine with fish. Edward waved at Hobbys, 'Here comes my physician again to take away all my pleasures, Hobbys, you are a plague on our conscience, and harder to please than our confessor, sit down and enjoy a glass of wine with one of these beautiful young ladies!'

Hobbys accepted the goblet, but declined the young lady with what he hoped was well concealed regret. She was very attractive and exposing much of her bosom as she bent over Hobbys giving him more wine, but how could he maintain his professional position and integrity if he succumbed to her freely offered luscious beauty in public. Hobbys wondered if he could perhaps see her afterwards, but discretion was sadly rare in Edward's palace.

# WESTMINSTER PALACE APRIL 8TH 1483

Edward lay in bed in the great state bedroom. He had collapsed at mass earlier in the morning, and been carried to his bed on a litter by six men required to manage his bulk. The room where he had made love to Elizabeth so many times, where some of his children had been conceived. Where Jane Shore had visited many times, and other women too numerous to remember. Now Edward lay in bed, pale, inert, his breathing rapid and shallow, with rattly noises from the secretions in his throat that he was too weak to cough up. Elizabeth sat by the bed holding his hand and weeping. Around the bed stood his daughters, Elizabeth, Cecily, Katherine, Anne, and Bridget. His son Richard, Earl of Shrewsbury, Duke of York stood at the back showing mixed emotions. What was happening to his father? The huge man who had dominated his short life. Could something awful happen to his father? What would happen to him and his brother if his father died? Tears ran silently down his cheeks.

Hobbys busied himself at the bedside, sharpening a knife before opening another of Edward's vein. Cupping so far had not helped; he must remove more blood, though Elizabeth Woodville watched in despair. 'Another King in another century will have to die from such primitive treatment before you doctors realise that it causes harm,' she said presciently looking distantly at the flames in the fire place.

'Your majesty, both the king's barber surgeon, Jacques Freis here, and I know this is the best therapy for the king. Bleeding has many benefits, we expect in this situation it will rid the blood of poisonous matter and cure the king's fever. It should clear his mind and feed his blood,' replied Hobbys.

'Then, pray tell we why you gave him cinnamon yesterday? I thought you only gave him that to increase his lust, not that it ever needed any assistance,' asked the Queen.

'Your majesty,' replied Hobbys, 'I gave him cinnamon in the past when he felt his bodily strength was poor, but cinnamon will also cure many infections, even the plague, and should always be given to any seriously ill person because of its extraordinary medical powers. For such an eminent man as our King, the cost is but a trifle.'

Elizabeth gave an exasperated sigh and sat again beside Edward's bed.

Edward's nobles stood around eying each other thoughtfully, suspiciously. Hastings and Dorset, the Stanley brothers wondering which faction they would support, usually one in each camp to maintain the family supremacy.

Elizabeth asked Hobbys, 'what do you think is wrong with him, what can you do'

Hobbys said, 'I am not sure, he does not appear worn out with old age, nor is he seized with any kind of malady known to me, therefore the cure does not appear easy in the case of a king or of a person of more humble rank.'

Hobbys turned to the king, 'your majesty, you must have a liquid diet to help your strength, can you drink a little milk, then some wine watered down to a quarter strength.' In the past the suggestion of little watered wine had generated some aggressive expletives, but Edward was too weak to do other than have a little sip, then fall back on his bed with his eyes still closed, apparently exhausted.

Later that evening Hobbys placed his hand on Edward's brow noting that he had developed a high fever. He also had a very rapid irregular pulse. Hobbys felt this was a bad sign. A draft of herbs was carefully poured down Edward's throat to lower his temperature.

Edward opened his eyes briefly and called weakly, "Where are my young brothers, England will need them to look after my son Edward when he is a young king, Edmund must be the Royal Protector, Richard must help, but Clarence is untrustworthy, where are they all?"

Hobbys was concerned that Edward had become delirious, it was over twenty years since Edmund was murdered, and five since Clarence had died.

Edward lapsed into a restless sleep, Hobbys sat beside the bed bleeding the king of another half pint of blood in the early hours, while the queen scowled at him. Hobbys noted that his pulse had become unusually slow. That was odd when it had been fast and irregular only a few hours before. Hobbys knew a slow pulse could be found with enteric fever. Something nagged in the recesses of his mind that could cause a pulse to vary so much, then it came to him, it was poisoning with the foxglove!

Hobbys had seen Margaret secreting some foxgloves only a few days ago! Could Margaret Beaufort have deliberately poisoned the king? Hobbys had never liked her, she always seemed to be plotting at one of her dark schemes. She had a superficial smile and always claiming a deeper spirituality than anyone else, but Hobbys saw her as a snake in the grass. Did she really think this would help her bastard son's chance of the throne?

In the morning Edward awoke, and spoke lucidly. He called Hastings and Thomas Grey, the Marquis of Dorset to his bedside, 'dear friends, I believe my time on this earth is about to end, for my sake and for my young son Edward, I beg you to solve your differences, and work together till the lad achieves manhood, for me shake hands and pledge yourselves to the young king. Where is Stanley, I would ask him the same favour, though he will always blows in the wind, wherever he sees advantage. One day he will back the wrong side and loose his head, but we need him for the present. Stanley must become the guardian to my daughter Elizabeth.'

Hastings leaned over the bed and extended his hand to Dorset, after a pause Dorset took the offered hand and gave it a perfunctory shake. Although it was said they both enjoyed the favours of Jane Shore, it seemed unlikely it would be at the same time, as they appeared mutually suspicious and antagonistic. Lord Stanley was not to be seen.

Edward pulled himself up, gathered his remaining strength and called for the queen to approach. 'My dearest wife, I thank you for all the happiness we have shared, and apologise for having strayed occasionally. I fear my time on earth is coming to a close. We must prepare for our son's minority, and therefore I appoint my loyal brother, Gloucester, to be the lord protector of our realm until young Edward becomes a man, no other person in the land has his status, a prince of the royal blood, no other person has shown the devoted loyalty Richard has displayed at my side in peace and war, he must hold the land together against those who would betray the House of York.'

Elizabeth was shocked, 'But my dear husband, Gloucester is unknown to our son, has little knowledge of London, or how to govern the kingdom, little Edward favours my brother, his guardian and mentor, Anthony Woodville, the Earl of Rivers, and also he trusts my son, your stepson, Thomas. Hastings and Stanley are familiar with the reins of government, together they would be a much better choice than Gloucester who only knows the north of England.'

The queen's brother, Lionel Woodville, the Bishop of Salisbury, equally shocked said, 'the queen is correct, Edward does not know Gloucester and trusts our family.'

'Enough! We have spoken, Richard has our full and unconditional love and trust.'

Edward collapsed back on his pillow, then spied Stanley lurking in the shadows at the back, a vulture just come in at the death to see what fine pickings were available. 'Thomas, my friend, we trust you will support my son and keep that wife of yours, Margaret Beaufort under close supervision, she still believes that her son, the son of two bastard lines, Henry Tudor has some right to the throne, though in this room and in our realm, there must be twenty or thirty with more royal blood than that lowborn opportunist.'

As the days progressed Edward lapsed back into delirium, raving about past battles, foes and friends as though they were all alive in the room, and he in the midst of battles, then lapsed into unconsciousness with increasing laboured irregular breathing which stopped and started again before finally ceasing in the evening as his family wept around the bed. Hastings bent over Edward and kissed his forehead, tears coursing down his cheek while Dorset and the queen looked at each other in silent understanding, and Stanley strode full of some intent from the room. He appeared neither surprised nor distressed.

Hobbys chewed his lip thoughtfully, worried about the effect this may have on his practice, after all Edward was by far his most important patient and greatest benefactor, it was not good for his reputation to have a relatively young man die in spite of his treatment. He wondered about the queen's comments about blood-letting, could she be correct, even John Argentine had agreed it was a good idea. He could see his practice amongst the nobles disappearing as faction fought faction, when he would be seen as Gloucester's man and physician. Hobbys though he would not trust any of them round the death bed with the realm, and was sure that Gloucester was the only person with the stature and integrity to control the Woodville's' grab for power.

Hobbys, as Sergeant Surgeon, was required to play a major part in the funeral rites. Edward's body was washed, the long veins opened and drained, and his orifices plugged. Edward then lay upon a board in Westminster Palace, his huge body naked except for a loin cloth, while the nobles, knights, bishops, major and aldermen filed past to pay their respects. The next day the body was then embalmed. Hobbys removed the internal organs and the body was then anointed with oils and spices, and wrapped with waxed linen cerements. The exposed head had a purple velvet cap of estate placed on it and red leather shoes were placed on the feet. Having performed his medical duties, Hobbys retired to his room to shed some quiet tears and reflect it was but five short years since the death of Clarence. Now three brothers all nominally under his care were dead. Should he have tried to be more forceful with Edward's overindulgence? His previous attempt had met with hostility. He must be careful to keep the forth brother in his apparent good health.

A day later Hobbys joined the queues filing past Edward's body in St Stephen's Chapel in Westminster where he lay in state for eight days, before the funeral service in Westminster Abbey and then the slow procession to St Georges Chapel in Windsor, where he would be buried twelve days later. Hobbys wondered to himself what was it inside Edward's vast frame, what had led to his death so young, could Elizabeth Woodville be correct that he had been bled too much. He should have opened up the heart when removing his vital organs before embalming to see if it was empty. Hobbys had only been following the standard management used by all his colleagues.

Three days after Edward's death on the 11th May, his elder son then at Ludlow two hundred miles from London, was proclaimed Edward V.

In the meantime strange rumours swirled around Westminster. Jacob visited Hobbys to share their observations and information. The council was dominated by the Wydville faction headed by the now dowager queen and her family, however a smaller faction led by Hastings and Stanley attempted to limit their power. Dorset and Hastings fell out totally when Hastings claimed possession of Jane Shore as his mistress. Messengers had been sent to Anthony Rivers at Ludlow to bring Edward, Prince of Wales to London for his coronation as soon as possible. 4th May was set as the provisional date for his coronation. Elizabeth Wydville and her son the Marquis of Dorset had seized the Tower and its treasure. Dorset had appointed his uncle, Sir Edward Wydville commander of the fleet to oppose either the French or hostile factions at home. Polydor Vergil was reputed to be saying that the king must have died of some secretive foul play, such as poisoning or sorcery.

Hobbys though such a statement may well be true. It implied some involvement of Elizabeth or Margaret Beaufort, though surely not in collusion. The dowager queen was too astute a political manipulator to be duped by Margaret's apparent support and grief.

The Wydville faction was determined to marginalise Richard of Gloucester and ignore the late king's appointment of him as protector, yet other rumours said that messengers had also been sent to Middleham, and that Richard was approaching with an army to battle the Wydville faction. Richard had found an important supporter in Henry Stafford, second Duke of Buckingham, a descendent of Thomas of Woodstock, the youngest son of Edward III. Buckingham grew up hating the Wydvilles having been compelled to marry Katherine Wydville, the Queen's sister when only eleven.

By the night of April 30th, it was clear that Gloucester and Buckingham had secured the future king, and that Rivers, Richard Gray, the king's half-brother and Thomas Vaughan; the king's chamberlain had been arrested and sent to remote castles under Gloucester's control.

The Wydville coup had failed. Gloucester and Buckingham paraded the young king through London on Sunday, May 4th. Gloucester's men followed the three bearers of the royal blood line, five hundred of them all dressed in black, and behind them were several cartloads of weapons, emblazoned with the Wydville crest, supposedly evidence that the Dowager Queen had plotted to raise an army against Gloucester, supplanting him as the young king's protector. However; Richard planned that his coronation should be soon, but that he, the Duke of Gloucester would be Lord Protector until Edward V reached adulthood.

# CROSBY'S PALACE, LONDON MAY 4TH, 1483

Catesby opened the door and admitted William, while Richard was undressed for his ablutions by his body servants.

'Master Hobbys, I know you served my father, the Duke of York, and my brother, our late king faithfully to the best of your ability for many years. I am sure that dear Edward would still be here, but for the Queen's family leading him into licentious paths. It would be a great source of comfort if you could care both for myself, and for my dear nephews, especially Edward, who seems in poor health. Physician John Argentine has seen him almost daily and waffles on in Latin about not very much saying that Edward is well when we all think the unfortunate boy looks sick, so although Argentine is supposed to be the top physician in the country, we would appreciate your opinion. You have more experience than Argentine.

Your position as royal physician will receive a grant of forty pounds a year. We must make him better before his coronation. We will conduct you to the royal apartments in the tower in a few days.'

'Your Grace, I loved your brother the king like a son, his death was a bitter blow to me, the dowager queen blamed me for his illness, but unfortunately he rarely followed my advice. He was too often persuaded by the queen's family to overindulge in the pleasures of life.' Hobbys replied while simmering inwardly, Argentine had persuaded everyone that he was the most knowledgeable physician in London, with his skeletal frame, hunched appearance hooked nose and dismissive stare as though others were not his intellectual equal, even though he qualified fairly recently and had nearly twenty years less experience than Hobbys. Argentine seemed to feel he could diagnose with his brilliant brain and proximity to God, and his reliance on examining phlegm, urine and stools without checking the whole body. Hobbys would be delighted to examine the young king, and show who was the best physician in town.

# JUNE 10TH 1483

Rumours around London suggested the dowager queen had attracted other nobles to her cause, and was endeavouring to raise another army which would out-number Gloucester's troop. In Baynard's castle, Gloucester turned to Catesby, accepted the quill and parchment offered, and wrote a letter while reading as he wrote, 'we heartily pray you to come unto us in London in all diligence ye can possible, after the sight hereof, with as many as ye can make defensibly arrayed, there to aid and assist us against the Queen, her blood, adherents and affinity, which have intended and do intend, to murder and utterly destroy us and our cousin, the Duke of Buckingham, and the old royal blood of this realm, and as it is now openly known, by their subtle and damnable ways forecasted the same.'

# THE TOWER OF LONDON, JUNE 11ᵀᴴ 1483

Richard, Henry Stafford, the Duke of Buckingham, and William Brandon strode purposefully through the tower gardens towards the royal apartments on south side of the white tower to be greeted by the constable of the tower. Hobbys followed close behind mesmerised by the power and menace of the old fortress, and indeed of the men leading him. However, Buckingham reminded Hobbys of George, Duke of Clarence. He was strikingly good looking and clothed in the most opulent attire. He appeared jovial and friendly, with many witty pronouncements, but there was something in his eyes suggesting a fickle character whose loyalty was shallow. Hobbys reflected Clarence was executed for treason when a little over the age of twenty-eight, if Stafford went down the same path at the same age, he would betray Edward V and Richard before the end of the year.

Many had entered here since the days of William the bastard and the Norman occupation to experience unbelievable pain before feeding the worms beneath his feet. Richard looked around puzzled, 'So William, where is Hastings?' he said, 'it is most important we should spend some time with the young king to check his health, and reassure him about the coronation. Hastings said he would be here with us, though I gather he took one look at Edward a day or two ago, and shot out of the Tower?'

'Your Grace,' responded Brandon, 'one of Hastings servants came to the palace at sunrise to say he was ill, and could not attend today.'

Richard frowned, 'Hastings has always been a loyal supporter of York, but his fondness for wine and women led my brother astray, and is not helping his health, I suspect that was the problem. What about Argentine, he was supposed to be here to discuss Edward's condition with Hobbys, where is he. Apparently he thought the King was unhappy, that he was seeing his chaplain for daily confession and penance, seeking remission of his sins in case anything happened to him, but Argentine didn't find anything wrong with his apart from a tooth infection or something similar. We should have had Hobbys here sooner for a second opinion, but the last month has been so busy controlling all the factions opposing us!'

Brandon shrugged his shoulders in ignorance. Guards sprang to attention and opened the doors to the sumptuous royal apartments. They passed through the banqueting hall of Edward I, and the audience chamber, into the privy chamber of the young king. Hobbys was overwhelmed by the stained glass windows depicting the royal arms and the fleur de lys, and the gold and vermilion tapestries and wall paintings portraying angels and birds. Hobbys briefly saw a young nearly grown man with blonde hair sitting waiting for their arrival.

William, Buckingham and Richard sank humbly to their knees, murmuring their, 'your majesty's,' and Hobbys followed hastily, clumsily, noting the floor tiles decorated with royal leopards, and the emblem of poor Richard II, the white hart. The apartment was opulent in the extreme as befitted the king of England.

Young Edward spoke, 'greetings uncle, it is always a pleasure to see you knowing how dear the role of royal protector is to you and to have your support until I am crowned.'

'Your Majesty, it is my pleasure and duty to serve you as I served your father, my dearly cherished brother Edward, our late lamented warrior prince. Today I come on another serious matter; I have brought Master William Hobbys with us. Hobbys was surgeon to your father for nearly twenty years, including on the French campaign serving him with great skill and compassion. Would that his advice had been followed a little more than that of your step-brother, Dorset. I can personally vouch for his integrity and ability. We would like him to consult you to ensure you are well on your coronation day.'

Hobbys looked at Edward's large feet, thinking he may be as tall as his father. Edward beckoned Hobbys saying, 'Master Hobbys, I thank you for all your care of my father the king. I am happy to accept you as my personal physician.'

Hobbys looked up. He opened his mouth saying, 'thank you, sire...' when he stopped dismayed, dumfounded by Edward's appearance. 'Oh no, Jesus, Mary and Joseph, Oh no, Oh no.'

Tears flooded down Hobbys face as Richard shook him, saying, 'pull yourself together man, what is the problem?'

Hobbys hesitated then regathered his composure somewhat, and stuttered to the young king.

'Your...your majesty, I had heard that your majesty has some problem with your jaw, may I examine your face to ensure that your grace is in excellent health for your coronation?'

Hobbys looked carefully at the red lump over Edward's jaw, noting a pale depigmented area in the middle. 'Your grace, is this painful when I press firmly?' Edward flinched a little, and confessed to mild discomfort, while endeavouring not to show pain in front of such doughty warriors as his uncle and Brandon. Hobbys pricked the pale central area with a sharp probe. 'Can you feel that your grace?' Edward shook his head. 'No Master Hobbys, I can't feel that at all.'

Hobbys, looking increasingly concerned, said, 'your majesty may I examine the rest of your body?' Hobbys rapidly observed some hypopigmented and hyperpigmented patches and some macular nodules over the trunk. Hobbys felt around Edward's elbows feeling some thickened cords just under the skin due to enlargement of the ulnar nerves. The bones in his hands were prominent due to wasting of the little muscles between them, and when Hobbys touched Edward's legs softly, gently, the prince was unable to feel his touch indicating numbness in the legs. Hobbys examination strongly supported his initial diagnosis, and added to his deepest despair. Argentine with all his astrological theory and reputation, his deep knowledge of theology, and air of omniscience, wasn't very good at examining his patients carefully. Hobbys was at a loss to understand why some thought Argentine was the best physician in the country.

Hobbys looked around the room; all eyes were on him, the faces of Gloucester, Buckingham, Brandon and Edward looking increasingly anxious at Hobbys distress.

Hobbys sank to his knees sobbing. 'My lords, it is my most grievous duty to tell you that I believe this to be leprosy, the red lumps over the jaw bone, in the neck and body with pale central depigmented numb areas, the thickened nerves in the elbow and the numbness in the legs, I believe they indicate leprosy. I believe we should obtain a second opinion on such a grievous diagnosis and suggest asking my colleague, master Fries to see the king at once.'

A shocked silence fell on the room.

After several minutes, Hobbys spoke again. 'My Lords, it is again my grievous duty to express my opinion as a physician, my lord Edward must be isolated until such time as he may recover with our prayers and God's will, though he may not recover. He cannot remain in the company of Prince Richard, nor your grace of Gloucester and the other nobles. He cannot be crowned king in his state of health and rule over us. I understand there are plans that his brother Richard the Duke of York should join him in the royal apartments soon. I cannot advise that. I suggest that my lord Edward be moved to St Giles leprosarium not far away, under a false name to protect his identity. I can only express an opinion on medical matters, not the great affairs of state.'

Edward fell back on the bed weeping, 'So you would put me, your rightful king in an isolation hospital, you would deny me the throne, and hope I die soon. Can I see my mother and brother?'

Gloucester, greatly distressed, said, 'your grace, we must protect your family, your nobles, your people, and we must treat your condition to the best of Master Hobbys ability. Perhaps should you recover by the grace of God, you could be restored.'

After another long pause, Richard spoke again. 'thank you Master Hobbys, we are all equally distraught at what you tell us, while we respect your skills, as you recommend, we would be desirous of a confirmatory opinion from one of your colleagues, perhaps master Fries as you suggest, otherwise you will not speak of this to anyone else on pain of death. You may leave us.'

Hobbys withdrew backwards, bowing, weeping. Edward sagged on his bed, all his authority suddenly stripped away. 'Why not stab me in the heart with your sword and finish me off quickly!' he sobbed.

Richard, the military commander, assumed control, he barked orders to Brandon and all around. 'Edward must be isolated from his brother and all of us immediately. Convey my nephew to the Bermondsey Abbey in Southwark across the river from here overnight. It has a history of caring for royalty, nearly fifty years ago Catherine de Valois, once the honourable wife of the great Henry V, honourable mother of the late King Henry VI, and dishonourable mother of Henry Tudor, lived there for some six months before her death. Joanna of Navarre, wife of the usurper Henry IV, lay in state there.'

'We will need the king's approval and signature on documents of state until alternative arrangements are made. Then arrange to place him in the Middlesex Hospital of St Giles for lepers under a false name, Hobbys you can accompany our Lord, Edward V to the hospital when I order. Ensure he receives the best of attention appropriate to his position and needs, ensure he has a bed for himself, not shared with other sufferers as is done in many hospital, though sharing with other lepers can scarcely hurt him now, and also ensure that he has a false name and is unknown.

Call my immediate circle of advisors including Bishop Stillington. Richard of Shrewsbury the Duke of York should be brought here to the royal apartments, though in different rooms. We must make plans to somehow crown him instead, somehow, sometime, we will have to inform everyone that Edward, the Prince of Wales is sick. We must pretend Edward is here and well until we can persuade Elizabeth Wydville, the Dowager Queen, to release Richard to us.'

Gloucester paused and thought for a while. 'We cannot announce the king's illness, but if we do not we, or more specifically I will be suspected of doing the king some harm. We will need a boy here to impersonate the king until the Duke of Yok is with us here in the royal apartments.'

A terrible anger suddenly overcame Richard. 'This is how Rivers cared for my nephew in Ludlow, he is to blame for Edward catching this scourge, we should disembowel him, mere beheading is too good for that upstart popinjay of base blood, nevertheless, send messengers to the Earl of Northumberland in Pontefract to try Rivers, Grey and Vaughan, confirm their guilt and have them executed immediately.' Richard's anger burnt with incandescent fury as he chewed his lower lip and twisted his ring round and around.

Sir Robert Brackenbury, The constable of the tower, spoke from the back of the room where he had remained quietly observing events, 'Your grace, my two daughters live in the tower in my apartments; they are aged thirteen and ten. Dressed as a boy, my Elizabeth, from a distance could appear to be the Prince of Wales.'

'Excellent, arrange that immediately,' replied Richard, 'we will meet here in a few days to address Richard of Shrewsbury, the Duke of York.'

# JUNE 13TH LONDON

Hobbys was seeing patients in Holborn when an outcry arose in the streets. Stepping outside he heard the news that Hastings had been executed after a council meeting. Richard had become suspicious that Hastings had encouraged him to spent time with a leper, while he had avoided a further meeting with the young king. His spies found Hastings had been plotting with the dowager queen, his previous adversary, to eliminate Gloucester. Hobbys was not surprised by the turn of events, though he feared Gloucester was making enemies and looking a brutal northern savage to the Londoners.

# JUNE 16<sup>TH</sup> 1483 THE ROYAL APARTMENTS IN THE TOWER OF LONDON

Hobbys leapt to his feet as Gloucester followed by Buckingham, Brandon and Brackenbury swept into the king's privy chamber. Young Richard, the Duke of York, also leapt to his feet, and ran to Richard, embracing him. 'Oh Uncle Richard, where is my brother Edward, the king, is he sick, what is happening?'

Gloucester glanced at Hobbys who had just finished his examination of Richard on the bed in the Royal Apartments. Hobbys nodded and said, 'The Prince is in perfect health your grace.'

Gloucester returned the boy's embrace, then sank to on knee before his nephew. 'Your grace, for so I must call you, I deeply regret having to tell you, your brother is mortally sick with leprosy. He has been taken to an isolation hospital and cannot become king. No one else must know the nature of his illness. Young Richard, my late brother's precious son, I must tell you that you are now the heir to the throne, we shall commence plans for your coronation.'

Richard of Shrewsbury looked totally dismayed. 'But Uncle Richard, I don't want to be king, Edward promised me he would be king. I want to be a doctor like Master Hobbys, I want to be Edward's doctor and make him and other people better.'

Gloucester smiled, 'Your grace, God does not always grant us our wishes, he gives us our duties, and we must all fulfil the role that he plans for us.'

Shrewsbury looked concerned. 'But uncle, my other uncle, the Duke of Clarence before he died, said Edward and I could never be King, because he was the rightful heir to the throne after my dear father.'

Gloucester smiled ruefully. 'Your grace, sadly my brother George was a tormented man, sometimes his ambition exceeded his family allegiance, he did say things like that, but they were not true.'

'Uncle Richard, Uncle George said we could not be kings and that he should because my father the king, was married to another lady before he married our mother.'

A stunned silence fell on the room, while those present assessed the significance of the little boy's casual remark. The smile disappeared from Gloucester's face, while he chewed his lower lip and twisted his wedding ring in thought.

Gloucester looked at his nephew with extreme anxiety, 'So my dear Prince Richard, do you remember any more details of what your uncle George said to you?'

Shrewsbury looked unconcerned, 'Uncle George used to smile at us sideways, but I don't think he liked us really. He once said when he thought we could not hear that he should have had more sons. I don't really remember exactly what he said, but I spoke to Edward last time we met in Westminster and Edward said that George told us that our father was betrothed to a lady called Eleanor and that the Bishop of Bath had performed the ceremony. Edward said not to tell anyone because he wanted to be king, but I don't, I want to be a king's physician.'

Silence descended on the room again. Gloucester gathered his thoughts, his brain whirling with the significance of this statement. 'Summon

Stillington, the Bishop of Bath and Wells to Westminster Palace immediately, we must have this clarified, Buckingham why are you kneeling before me?'

'Because your grace,' replied Buckingham, taking Richard's hand, 'you are the rightful monarch, neither Edward's nor George's children can now inherit the throne, you have more Plantagenet blood in your veins than anyone else in the country, well except possibly me. You are my king!' Buckingham kissed Richard's ring. Gloucester looked at him in shock, Buckingham's comment about his own Plantagenet blood did not escape him. Gloucester said 'We must call the royal council and consider matters. Dear young Richard, I had only wanted to be the king's general and also keep you all safe. We need you to go somewhere safe while this is all sorted out, Brackenbury, your other daughter can masquerade as Richard in the Tower royal apartments.'

'Uncle Richard,' spoke his nephew, the only person totally happy with the turn of events, 'perhaps I could stay with my Aunt Margaret in Burgundy, she said she has a page boy, called Perkin, who is my age and looks exactly like the portrait of me send to her last Christmas. Perhaps I could play with him, if I can't see my poor brother.'

Richard continued his plans for the future, 'Brackenbury, I thank you for your offer of your two daughters to impersonate my two nephews while we try to find the truth of Richard's story and make plans for the future. You are appointed constable of the tower from this day. There must be two children here at all times to appear as though they are the princes, but they can stay in the inner chamber here, and only be seen from a distance. I expect people will think I have done something terrible to them should I follow Buckingham's suggestion. Oh, Mary, mother of God, what is the rightful and honourable course for me? Had Rutland survived there would be two of us to sort out this mess, he perhaps could have been king, and I could remain the king's general. Buckingham, my dear cousin, send my dear nephew Richard to my sister in Burgundy as soon as possible. I will write a letter outlining these terrible events to her, but it must be for her eyes only.'

# WESTMINSTER PALACE JUNE 17ᵀᴴ 1483

Robert Stillington, the former Lord Chancellor, still the bishop of Bath and Wells entered to see a furious Duke of Gloucester scowling at him. Brackenbury, Lovell and Buckingham all looked equally angry.

'So my lord bishop, do you have anything to tell me about my late brother, King Edward and Eleanor Butler, something you should have told me weeks ago?' asked Gloucester.

Stillington bowed, and then sank to his knees. 'My lord of Gloucester, I had plans to come and see you today, when your summons arrived. This matter has weighed on my conscience for all these years. Only yesterday I was taking the confession of Margaret Beaufort, though the saintly lady never has anything to confess, not that I can tell you more about that.'

Gloucester glanced at his colleagues, they all looked at each other, then back to the bishop, their expressions suggested that they all shared the same thought; they all felt Margaret was not as saintly as she professed and that she would be up to one of her secret conspiracies.

'Margaret told me she had heard the rumours about Eleanor Butler, how she hears so much is beyond me, and asked if it was true. We ended up with me confessing to her, which is perhaps appropriate, I feel she has a closer relationship with the Almighty than I do, she lives such a holy life,' continued Stillington.

Richard chewed his lip and twirled his ring in frustration, more likely she had a close relationship with the devil. 'Come on man, what do you have to tell us?'

Stillington replied, 'Your Grace, Margaret was insistent that I should tell you this story, she said she feared for my immortal soul if I did not tell you all immediately.'

Richard scowled, what was Margaret up to, if Edward Prince of Wales and Richard of York could not become king, then who did Margaret think would be next in line, not that Welsh bastard her son, what was her game? Did she foresee that if he took the throne himself, he would appear a usurper, even a murderer of his brother's sons, that it might alienate some of his supporters? How could Stillington confuse Margaret for a saint when she could hatch such a devious plot? The bishop appeared unable to distinguish the angel Gabriel from the fallen angel Lucifer, a more likely role for Margaret.

Stillington confessed all the details, that he presided over a pre-nuptial ceremony between Edward and Eleanor, that Edward seemed in an almighty hurry to get through the ceremony only to disappear with Eleanor for an hour.

Richard thought briefly and asked very quietly, though none could doubt his anger and the implied threat, 'so my Lord Bishop, is that why Edward stripped you of the position of Lord Chancellor, and why were you jailed at the time of my brother George's trial, Stillington, did you tell George?'

Stillington fell flat on his face and sobbed, 'my Lord, the Duke of Clarence persuaded me that he needed to confess, then held a knife to my throat in the confessional, under such duress I told him all, my Lord, I am not a fighting man.'

'Get out,' shouted Richard and the bishop scuttled for the door as fast as his fat legs would carry him.

Anthony Wydville, the Earl Rivers, Sir Richard Haute, Sir Richard Grey, the half-brother of Edward V, and Sir Thomas Vaughan were all executed in Pontefract Castle on 24th June.

# LONDON, JULY 1483

Hobbys returned to his London practice, for a week or two he received no summons to the Palace of Westminster. He kept a solemn silence about his terrible diagnosis in the tower. Martin Fries independently had reached the same conclusion as Hobbys. The rumour going around London was that Robert Stillington, the Bishop of Bath and Wells, had been summoned before Gloucester to reveal that he had presided over the betrothal of Edward IV to a lady called Eleanor Butler, the daughter of John Talbot, the Earl of Shrewsbury, the widow of Sir Thomas Butler in 1461. Apparently she refused to bed with him unless they were married, hence immediately after the ceremony Edward and Eleanor had retired to an adjacent room for a half hour, and returned with both parties appearing dishevelled but contented. That would not surprise Hobbys, considering his first meeting with Elizabeth Wydville nearly twenty years ago. There was no record of Edward and Eleanor ever meeting again, and Eleanor died in 1468, having retired to a convent, perhaps feeling jilted. There were even rumours of the couple having a child. From Hobbys experience this was quite a plausible story, but the problem was that Eleanor was alive when Edward married Elizabeth Wydville, making him a bigamist, and their marriage invalid, as was the claim of Edward's children to the throne.

Events progressed inevitably to Gloucester accepting the throne. Hobbys received an invitation to the coronation as he had expected, but on arriving at Westminster Abbey, he was turned back from the front entrance where the nobles and leading members of London society were admitted, to the back entrance where the gentry and merchants of London were allowed entrance to the rear of the congregation. Not for the first time, Hobbys felt there was some mistake, surely he as the king's doctor should be among the more important citizens near the front. Not only was he a highly trained expert with a doctorate from Cambridge, without his diagnostic skills, it could have been Edward V being crowned, though his leprosy would soon have become apparent to Dr. Argentine and any blind man with some common sense. Had that happened, Gloucester could have been imprisoned, even executed by the Wydville faction, and Buckingham would still be a minor noble of little account rather than the holder of the king's train, and the second most important man in the land. Surely Buckingham would receive a stack of benefits and titles after the coronation, though Hobbys suspected there was really only one title that he though Buckingham desired, and believed he was worthy of, that of king!

Hobbys refocussed on events in front of him. Hobbys watched as the new king and his queen, Anne followed the Duke of Norfolk, now the Earl Marshall and High Steward, Buckingham, the Duke of Suffolk carrying the sceptre, Suffolk's son John, the Earl of Lincoln carrying the orb, and the Earl of Surrey carrying the sword of state. Richard was supported by Stillington, and Anne's train was carried by Margaret Beaufort, now Lady Stanley. Margaret appeared to be sneering at everyone ahead of her. Strangely Hobbys could not see Cecily Neville, the new king's mother anywhere.

Then Richard was to receive the anointing, the most sacred part of the ceremony. As he knelt at the high altar, his robes were removed, revealing a silk shirt lowered just below his shoulders. A new monarch was expected to reveal his body. The Archbishop of Canterbury anointed him on the head, the shoulders, the back above the shirt and on the elbows. Then Richard accepted the royal regalia, the crown, sceptre and rod. Richard's shirt had been carefully lowered just a little so his spinal curvature was not visible. Four of his knights of the Garter held a pall just above his head, so the congregation saw little of Richard's upper body. Hobbys did not know if they all were aware of Richard's scoliosis, but they all did a good job of concealing it from the flock.

What a nest of vipers thought Hobbys, Lord and Lady Stanley, and Buckingham. Surely Richard could recognise a collection of Brutus's. After the ceremony, the nobility retired to Westminster Hall, strangely Hobbys thought, his invitation did not include the banquet.

Rumours abounded about the princes in the tower. Hobbys told no one, not even his former wife Alice, especially not wife Alice, she would have told the whole neighbourhood, and Hobbys would have appeared before an increasingly grim Richard of Gloucester, now Richard III.

The king and queen departed for a royal procession in July, which included the investiture of their only son, Edward of Middleham as the Duke of York in York Minster on 8th September. Richard ordered a Crownswearing event in addition, an old tradition commencing with Edward the Confessor when the people could see the crowned monarch, and the nobles could pledge allegiance. Previously this had been held in Gloucester, Westminster and Winchester at key dates in the Church Calendar, but Richard wanted crownswearing in his beloved city of York, and needed to cement his position as soon as possible.

The 'princes' were seen in the tower less and less, and there were never any reports of them being seen after 29th September, perhaps Brackenbury had taken them back to his home, though Richard had ordered that there should be children there indefinitely appearing to be the two princes.

# HOLBORN 13TH OCTOBER 1483

A dusty, breathless and sweaty soldier bearing the arms of Richard III, swung off his horse and hammered on the door of Hobbys home. 'Come on man', he cried when Hobbys opened his door, 'Your king has need of your skills immediately. The foul traitor Buckingham has rebelled against his majesty, and a battle is imminent. Pack your equipment and follow on your cart to the West Country, aim for Salisbury where you should meet up with the Royal army.' Hobbys reached Salisbury after two weeks of travel through muddy roads and torrential rain, hearing rumours along the way, that Henry Tudor was planning to land with an invading army. However by the time Hobbys caught up with Richard's army, Buckingham had been apprehended in Beaulieu Abbey, and brought to Salisbury where he was rapidly and publically beheaded on 2nd November. Richard refused to see him. News followed shortly that the Tudor had attempted a landing on the same day, and fled in terror on hearing of the collapse of Buckingham's rebellion and the proximity of loyal troops.

Richard summoned Hobbys to the Royal Tent shortly after the execution. 'Ah Master Hobbys, we thank you for your loyal attendance on our soldiers, sadly Buckingham, the most untrue creature living, or he was living a little while ago, could not even provide us with a small battle. This royal duke will be paid some respect in death, more than he deserves, so he will not be available for your studies, instead he will be buried immediately there in the yard of the Blue Boar Inn. We have other duties for you Master Hobbys, we have no wounds for you to treat, nor any bodies for your knife here, however a small skirmish between my leading scouts and a few brave men-at-arms under Buckingham occurred west of here, and I am told there are some casualties in Sherborne Abbey without medical aid. Please take you wagon and your skills to attend them before returning to London. I shall provide you with four of my men with horses to enable you to traverse these muddy roads.'

Richard always respected the common soldier after a battle, no matter which side he fought upon, indeed they often had little choice in which army they fought.

The King continued, 'Rest assured we shall have much more sport for you when that base renegade, Tudor finally summons up enough courage to land on our shores. You can have his bastard body for whatever you please. I suspect you will find little evidence of manhood. Do you have any other news for me about another of your customers?'

'Your Majesty,' said Hobbys, again on his knees, 'I carried out your orders to the letter, conditions were as satisfactory as possible, and since that day, I have not revisited, nor heard any news from the source. As always I am your loyal servant, I shall proceed to Sherborne, then back to London to be ready to assist you on the battlefield, or back at Westminster.'

'And indeed you shall,' cried Richard, 'you will accompany my army when we re-enter London in triumph, with all the untrue rebels vanquished.'

# SHERBORNE OCTOBER 1483

A day and a half later, Hobbys pulled up just outside the magnificent Benedictine Abbey, an old monastic school, where Alfred the Great was educated as a child, and where the bones of two of his brothers, Aethelbald and Ethelbert, both kings of Wessex, were reputed to be buried. Hobbys walked into the nave through the west door. Glancing up, he saw, as he had heard, that it was decorated with some of the most beautiful fan vaulting in Europe. A dozen men lay on straw pelisses on the floor, all had severe wounds, were pale, blood stained and in pain. Most still wore some armour. A lady was feeding them some gruel, otherwise they appeared to have been ignored.

A small crowd of locals watched quietly unwelcoming from a corner. Hobbys was shocked to hear mutterings about bloody Norman scum, getting what they deserved. Hobbys was surprised to hear such comments still, hatred of the Norman occupation had died out over a hundred years ago or more in most places, but clearly here old memories died hard, and any man in armour recalled the most feared and ferocious knights in Christendom, and their atrocious barbaric treatment of the Anglo-Saxons for a couple of centuries. In Sherborne, the Normans were more hated than most places, their beautiful Saxon church was destroyed, though its successor was even more magnificent, and its importance as the capital of Wessex in Alfred's time was totally lost. The Norman's wished to portray themselves a race of civilised cultured men, compared with the primitive Anglo-Saxon savages living in mud huts, to proclaim that the Battle of Hastings was a blessing for the English, but here the truth was still recalled very differently.

Hobbys and his apprentices washed and dressed wounds, provided laudanum, amputated a leg for one poor man whose lower leg was broken, with most of the flesh stripped of the bone. Another man lay groaning under a blood stained cloth. Gently removing the cloth, Hobbys saw a deep wound in the abdominal wall, with smelly red and brown liquid seeping out. 'What is your name?' he asked.

The man croaked hoarsely in reply, 'Will'.

'Will, what happened to you, poor fellow?' Hobbys asked.

'I was shot with an arrow,' he replied, 'I pulled it out, but it still is very painful.'

The smell suggested to Hobbys that he was gut shot as the Vikings used to call it, in which case he would surely die shortly. Hobbys used an old Viking trick to confirm the diagnosis. Before battles he made up a bottle of boiled leeks and onions in a thick soup. He spooned a little into the unfortunate man's mouth and returned a few minutes later to smell the wound. In addition to the previous odour, he could clearly smell onions in the discharge from the wound. The arrow had clearly penetrated the man's intestines and he had virtually no chance of survival. Hobbys gave more laudanum and a liberal quantity of wine, till the man lapsed into unconsciousness. By the next morning he had died, as had three others. The remainder, Hobbys loaded onto his cart, and left the old town to some unwelcome comments from the townsfolk.

Two months later, Hobbys was told his position as king's physician to Richard was officially confirmed, again with an income of forty pounds a year, though now this was for life as a token of appreciation for his many years of service to the house of York. Whispers in court from one of the clerks informed Hobbys that the money came from fines paid to the crown in Bedford and Buckingham, oh well, what did it matter where it came from, thought Hobbys.

# HOLBORN 1484

Hobbys heard with all of London that Richard called a Parliament on 23rd January to pass an act confirming his right to the throne in favour of his nephews because Edward's marriage to Elizabeth Wydville was not legal, and shortly after his son Edward of Middleham was declared heir to the throne, however only a few weeks later he died suddenly, a year to the day that Edward IV died, on April 9th. The cause of his death was unknown, Hobbys never had a chance to see him as his illness was so acute. Some reports said he had severe abdominal pain. Richard and Anne were reported to be distraught beyond all measure. They never had a second child, and the queen had always appeared pale and thin to Hobbys, not the robust child-bearing body of the dowager queen.

# OCTOBER 1484

**A** thunderous knock on the door disturbed Hobbys morning surgery. Hobbys' assistant opened the door to find a soldier dressed in the arms of England and a most distinguished gentleman wearing a gold edged black velvet cape. 'Summon master Hobbys immediately in the name of the king,' ordered the gentleman.

Hobbys peering over his associate's shoulder, bowed low, "My lord, William Catesby, how may I be of service to you?'

'Our lord, Richard III, demands your presence in Westminster Palace, her majesty the queen is unwell, and he would like your care and opinion. Personally, I suggested that Dr Argentine should attend the Queen as the most eminent doctor in the land, but the king recalls your past assistance and desires your attendance.'

Hobbys bowed low concealing a scowl. 'I shall collect my equipment and be in the Palace within the hour'. Would he have to tolerate this erroneous perception that Argentine was a competent clinical doctor, rather than a self-important expert in theology and astrology.

Hobbys arrived at Westminster, and was ushered directly to the queen's chamber in the royal apartments where a group of earnest young physicians, quills and parchment at the ready to record any gems of information, were gathered around Dr Argentine. Queen Anne lay on her bed surrounded by her ladies-in –waiting headed by a very contented looking Margaret Beaufort.

John Argentine surveyed his fellow physicians over his long nose, his back curved beyond his years, although some twenty years younger than Hobbys, he looked as old, with the gravitas of his widely accepted role as the foremost physician scholar in England. Argentine looked up noticing Hobbys with a transient expression of irritation. 'Ah, my dear young colleagues, this is Master Hobbys, a barber-surgeon with considerable skill in knowing why his patients died.' Hobbys was discomforted by the laughter, vowing to himself that he would not leave this room without obtaining some revenge.

'Why Argentine, what a surprise to see you back in England, how was the Tudor, still skulking in Paris, afraid to return to England? Someday I may inform you of an obvious diagnosis you missed in an eminent person before running away to France. Did you finally decide that there was perhaps more future for you here than supporting that illegitimate claimant to the English throne?'

'Why Hobbys, I have been in the University of Sorbonne, studying medicine and theology. Cassiterides has little to offer to a physician of my knowledge, though I doubt you know where that is. I even heard Erasmus lecture and suggested to him that he should spend time in Cambridge University. I also went to Padua, the great university centre of medical knowledge, and I went to the Basilica of St Anthony. You may not have heard of him Hobbys, during your visits to Southwark, but he is known as the doctor of the church. Among his miracles, he was able to reattach a boy's amputated leg, and heal it, and to return a murdered man to life, a bit more skilled that chopping up dead people you may think, but do not worry Hobbys, the Vatican has no plans to canonise you. Incidentally I never saw Henry Tudor. Let me continue my examination.'

Hobbys replied,' why my dear Argentine, anyone with a basic knowledge of ancient Greek knows that Cassiterides is the Scilly Isles, though many of limited understanding believe it to represent all the isles of Britain.' He wished he had brought his rapier and could call Argentine out.

Hobbys watched carefully looking for any other errors he could expose. He thought Argentine's approach was rather theological and academic but showed a lack of wide experience, and respect for those with greater familiarity with diverse diseases. Argentine peered at the two flasks containing bloody sputum and cloudy urine, samples collected from Queen Anne. 'Gentlemen, you may not be aware that Hippocrates of immortal memory, though not a Christian, as he lived a little before our Saviour, thought the expectoration of blood was due to a condition called phthisis, otherwise known as the white plague, a wasting disease, sadly nearly always fatal. Phthisis is of course derived from the Greek word, 'phthien' meaning to waste away.'

Hobbys raged inwardly at his patronising attitude, but was not about to be belittled. 'My dear Argentine, on this occasion you are correct, your knowledge of medicine is quite good for a man with only a master's degree, Hippocrates was born some four and a half centuries before Christ, and I am sure we are all familiar with his texts, *On the Physician* and *The Complicated Body* in which he also described the swelling of the terminal digit of the fingers called drumstick fingers, which you may perhaps have noticed the Queen also shows. Hippocrates thought this was due to chronic suppuration. Her urine sample appears cloudy but not pungent.'

'Precisely my dear boy, and incidentally after my studies at Eton and then the elite universities of Cambridge, Strasbourg and Padua, my studies for the Doctorate of Divinity are far advanced. We all know the D.D is a higher degree than M.D.' interjected Argentine, surreptitiously looking across the room at the bed where Anne lay inertly to check her finger nails.

Hobbys continued, fuming internally, 'Hippocrates thought phthisis, or consumption as it is usually known in England today, was a hereditary disease. He did not distinguish between a contagious disease running in a family, and a hereditary condition.'

'My dear colleague, young Master Hobbys also correctly identified the cloudy urine without any offensive smell, suggesting kidney disease without infection, probably caused by a severe chest condition. Hippocrates recommended milk therapy for phthisis.'

'Ass's er milk is what Argentine is referring to,' added Hobbys.

Argentine continued undistracted to display his superior knowledge, 'Aretaeus of Cappadocia recognised the association of phthisis with blood in the sputum in the second century after the birth of our Lord Jesus Christ. Galen, the physician to Marcus Aurelius in 174 AD, also advised milk therapy, so we should include that in our recommended treatment.'

Hobbys added, 'Galen was the first to notice lung nodules on post-mortem examinations, often an important procedure to diagnose the problem, and protect others.' Hobbys could have added that it was breast milk that was recommended, he speculated to himself that getting consumption was not that bad if the treatment could be taken directly from Jane Shore! Galen had also recommended wolf's liver, elephant's urine and sea voyages, Hobbys thought he could do better!

'Argentine omitted the recommendation of Tertullian at about the same time of boiled butter with honey, he may not be aware of that recommendation.' Hobbys was gratified to see the group of physicians taking notes of his pronouncements and looking at him with respect. 'Avicenna also supported treatment with honey.' Hobbys concluded, with a triumphal glance at Argentine, who was studiously ignoring him. He continued, 'And my dear colleague, Argentine, it is recommended that physicians should bath regularly and smell pleasantly scented. I expect without a wife to look after you and ensure adequate lavage, you are unaware of your personal odour. May I recommend rose petals in the bath, since a man of your character is unlikely to please a woman enough to want to be your wife.'

Argentine paused looking down his nose at Hobbys, 'my dear colleague, if I had the time, and the morals of an alley cat, I perhaps could attend the stews of Southwark, and enjoy scented baths with the ladies there.'

Dismissing the topic, Argentine perused the queen's horoscope compiled by the astrologer, implying unhappiness and sorrow, a death and problems in a marriage. 'My dear colleagues,' Argentine said learnedly, peering down his nose, 'the impending conjunction of Saturn and Jupiter is often a portent of death, which alas may occur here.' The fact that the Queen was distressed on hearing his comments passed Argentine's notice. Hobbys thought this was a load of rubbish, it did not take a horoscope to see the queen's distress over her many relatives who had died from war or disease, her incurable sorrow at the death of her only child, and her sorrow at being unable to provide the king with another heir.

Thomas Bemmersley, her physician in Middleham who had attended the birth of her Edward, added, 'When her Majesty gave birth she was severely damaged such that I thought she would never be able to carry a child again.'

Collectively the gathering of physicians and surgeons around the table had all noticed the queen's persistent cough, her skeletal figure, she appeared to be only skin and bone, her pallor and her expression of despair and sorrow. Martin Freis, one of Hobbys dear colleagues, a doctor of common sense and broad experience, with none of Argentine's self-importance and airs and graces, articulated what we were all thinking. 'We must thank our two eminent colleagues for their cultured debate, so full of wisdom and courtesy, and return to the problem before us. So we all think the poor lady has phthisis, then his grace the king, must never cohabit with her again. Her treatment should clearly include milk and honey.'

# JANUARY 1484 WESTMINSTER PALACE

Three months passed, the queen's doctors gathered for their weekly visit to the clearly sinking lady. Rumours had passed around of Elizabeth of York, the eldest daughter of Edward IV being enamoured of the king. Hobbys disbelieved these rumours, after all rumours went around about his own liaisons and not all of them were true.

They had discussed treatments, honey, liquorice and figs, milk and white meat, however all therapies had been tried already without success, and Anne was now refusing most food and drink. She appeared to have a death wish, she appeared to feel that Richard's only path to an heir was remarriage after her death.

Hobbys looked at Argentine. 'Well dear John, since Richard has asked you to convene this group, and he perceives that you are the foremost physician in England, you are the man to convey our opinion to the king.'

'Oh no,' prevaricated Argentine, 'dear William, you are known by all your colleagues as being especially skilled in matters of death. How will I look as being unable to cure the queen in spite of my status, dear William, your reputation is not as illustrious as mine, and you have known the king for two decades. He does have some trust in your judgement for reasons that are quite obscure to me, I am sure you should inform the king.'

Hobbys found himself seething with anger at Argentine yet again, however it was his duty to convey the news, good or bad, to the king.

Richard could usually see straight through hypocrisy, and would work out why Hobbys had to break the news, once he had overcome his anguish at his physicians' suggestions .Argentine reminded him in ways of the mythological Caladrius bird, he was very pale with prematurely white hair, his nose was a big as a bird's beak, and like the bird, he would never look a dying person in the face, or as it appeared their nearest relative. Also the Caladrius bird was said to mate faithfully for life, a desirable virtue Hobbys regretfully had never mastered. Hobbys couldn't see Argentine being interested in the pleasures of the flesh, or indeed anyone being interested in bedding Argentine. However the similarity was probably incorrect as the bird was supposed to be a creature of great beauty.

Rotherham, the Archbishop of York, accompanied Hobbys to the Royal Chambers. Richard looked even more a man broken by the cares of the world, but sat in silence on hearing the news. Rotherham attempted to put a positive view on events, 'Your Majesty, you would be advised to seek a new consort to bear you a son, now her majesty is grievously stricken with a short time to live and carries a dangerous infection, I am sure the church would support an application for a divorce.'

Richard looked up sharply, 'get out,' he said softly, but menacingly, distress written all over his face.

Later that night Richard summoned Hobbys and said, 'Master Hobbys, you have served my family for three generation for three decades, please see the queen daily, treat her to the best of your ability as we know you will, report to me daily of her condition while we are here, and always daily assure her of my love and concern, finally if you find us together, keep that to yourself and do not reprimand us as you did my brother, for we care little for this life anymore. We shall look forward one day to being united again with our father, brothers, and son.'

Hobbys was aware of the palace rumours that Richard was poisoning his wife, and that he intended to marry his niece. While the true state of a marriage is only known by the two involved, Hobbys knew Richard well enough to see his deep inward grief at Anne's steady deterioration. Richard turned the ring on his little finger round and round in silence, then said, 'The brothers of York should be riding high across the country, Edward as a still young king, with Edmund, George and myself as his most loyal warriors and wisest councillors, yet I am the only one left.' The amnesia of time had raised even Clarence to the status of a loyal warrior in Richard's dreams. 'My brother will be recalled as one of the great warrior kings of England, with Arthur and Alfred, with Edward I and Edward III, yes even Henry V, greater than William the bastard, for Edward was loved by his people. Yet his prowess on the battlefield was expended righting the wrongs imposed on this country by the usurpation of Henry IV.'

Richard paused and continued wistfully, 'but for that we would not have walked in triumph through London and Tewksbury, but through the gates of Paris, or even the gates of Jerusalem.'

Richard took a melancholy sip from his goblet of claret and continued, 'how has it come to a stage where a base born Welshman is perceived as a possible king. His maternal great-great grandfather, John of Gaunt, may not have been the son of Edward III. The king did not attend his birth as he did for his other sons. His maternal grandfather John Beaufort was the child of the adulterous relationship of John of Gaunt and Katherine Swynford. Their offspring were barred from accession to the throne. His paternal grandfather may have been Owen Tudor, a lowborn Welshman, or it may have been Edmund Beaufort, the first Duke of Somerset having an adulterous relationship with the dowager queen. His paternal grandmother, the dowager Queen Catherine, widow of Henry V, had no English Royal blood, and her relationships occurred without royal approval. Henry Tudor's predecessor as Lancastrian claimant to the throne, Edward of Lancaster, was probably the result of Margaret of Anjou illegitimate coupling with Edmund Beaufort, the third Duke of Somerset. Those Beauforts appear to have a penchant for dipping the quills in a king's inkwell, a crime usually punishable for instant execution.

The Tudor's father and uncle, while half-brothers to Henry VI, were not considered eligible to be in line to the throne, and his mother, that tenacious viper, also comes from the illegitimate Beaufort line. It was Margret Beaufort who ensured Stillington came forward with the information about Edward and Eleanor Butler being betrothed, now she claims I am a murderous usurper! Never has a claimant to the English throne come from a blood line so tainted by bastards and adulterers, may they all burn in hell'

Richard paused for a few minutes looking reflectively into the fire, then resumed, 'My predecessor as the Duke of Gloucester, Humphrey, brother of Henry V, a warrior king, was furious that Owen should have been so presumptuous to intermix his blood with the noble race of kings, and Humphrey was a Lancastrian! Even when Henry IV legitimised the offspring of Gaunt's adulterous affair with Katherine Swynford, he added a proviso that the Beaufort line should never never succeed to the English throne, yet the Tudor claims the throne as a Lancastrian! It is said that the Tudor was baptised as Ywain after one of his possible grandfathers, no Englishman would accept a king with that Welsh name, and then Margaret changed it to Henry to sound like the Lancastrian Kings. Everything about the man is false, his blood lines is tainted for many generations!'

'Yet Master Hobbys, once before a bastard pretender to the throne came to this country from France, and through sheer good luck managed to defeat Harold Godwinson at the Battle of Hastings after Harold had won the previous Battle of Stamford Bridge against Harald Hardrada and his treacherous brother Tostig. Treacherous brothers can pull a family down, had George been loyal throughout, my brother Edward would have held the throne easily without all the stress he suffered, and may still be alive.'

'Anyway, that Norman bastard from France almost destroyed this country with his barbaric subjugation of the poor Anglo-Saxon people. He knew nothing of English culture and traditions, the beauty of its people and their country, the legal rights of all folks, and the position of women in society. He wanted only power, titles and the people's taxes. It took several centuries before the Normans became absorbed and accepted into England. My brother and I are the first English kings to have four English grandparents for centuries. Let us pray that God provides us success against this French Tudor bastard for the good of our people, for he would be another Norman, taxing the people and curbing their rights, but one without proven courage in battle.'

Richard sat quietly for a while, and then said, 'Hobbys, have you heard of the Middleham Jewel? It is an exquisitely crafted gold religious icon. It used to belong to Anne Beauchamp, my mother-in-law. When my wife was expecting our beloved son, she gave it to Anne, as it provided religious and perhaps magic protection during childbirth, and we all remained well for several years, till it disappeared from Middleham Castle when I was away several years ago. It may sound improbable to you, but it was a religious icon, an engraved pendant believed to bring good luck and health to the owner. It was twice as long as my thumb. On one side it had a beautiful engraving of the crucifixion, depicting God supporting his son, our Lord Jesus on the cross, with a dove above to represent the Holy Spirit. On the other side was a nativity scene. Jesus is lying in a crib while Mary kneels beside him in adoration. They are surrounded by saints who had assisted with the birth of Jesus, and by Joseph watching, along with an ox and an ass. Around the crucifixion scene was written in Latin *'behold the Lamb of God, that takest away the sins of the world. Have mercy on us.'* The back could be slid aside to reveal a piece of material said to be from our Lord's shroud. Ever since it disappeared the family of York have suffered death and disease, George, Edward, my little Edward and now Anne. Someone has it and has cursed us.'

Richard lapsed back into silent meditation briefly and continued, 'Things of beauty are really only beautiful if they can be shared. No longer can I hold my loved one in my arms. No longer will we awake to the sound of our son's laughter. The pleasures in life are progressively deserting me.' Richard looked down at his hands, twisted Warwick's silver ring around and chewed his lip before continuing, 'Master Hobbys, your position enables you to read men's faces, and how do you read my Lord of Stanley? Normally I can see loyalty or treachery written on a man's face. With Stanley I see only an opportunist, sometimes with eyes wide open, sometimes half closed and calculating, but always considering what advantage he may gain from any situation. If I looked into Satan's eyes I would have a clearer idea of what he was planning. Tell me if you have any useful information about what motivates him, would you.'

'My Lord, Stanley is loyal to himself, he did not tell the truth about the sad death of little Prince George, blaming me when he refused to protect the little boy as I ordered, I would not trust him. If I hear any news of his treachery, I shall tell you immediately.' Hobbys bowed in allegiance and quietly withdrew. He reflected that Richard had a severe dose of melancholia, usually caused by an excess of black bile.

As the king requested, Hobbys visited Anne daily, he tried all the remedies from his ancient texts, including a mixture of laurel leaves and red wine, but Anne showed no will to live, no wish for food, and only accepted a minimal amount of nutritious food.

Her condition deteriorated very slowly with increased haemorrhages from her lung. The king appeared overwhelmed by the series of unhappy events happening round him, the Tudor had been welcomed into the French court of King Charles, John de Vere, the only battle hardened general left in the Lancastrian camp, had escaped and crossed the channel to join the gathering of rebels around Tudor, and a William Collingbourne had been hung, drawn and quartered for pinning a treasonous note on the door of St Pauls.

Anne finally died on 16th March. There was an eclipse of the sun that day. Many said it was a foretelling of the eclipse of the Yorkists. Nine days later Hobbys sat near the front for her funeral service in Westminster Abbey. She was buried near the tomb of Sebert, a former king of the East Saxons.

The King was inconsolable, he wept openly though Norfolk, Brackenbury and Lincoln tried to comfort him. As he prepared to walk out leaving the love of his life for ever, he spotted Hobbys and walked over to him. Hobbys sank to his knees fearing the worst, exile, torture, even beheading, however Richard grasped his hand and drew him to his feet, his eyes revealing a pain beyond any of Hobbys medications. 'Thank you caring for the queen, there is no doctor in the land who could have given her more expert treatment than you. I will be needing your services on the battlefield before the year is out, perhaps if all goes well you will be able to dissect that base-born Tudor pretender to our throne to see how little heart he has.' Richard patted Hobbys on the back and left. Hobbys preened himself, what a shame Argentine was not in the Abbey to hear an accurate assessment of the pecking order in medicine in England!

Daily the king looked more careworn, he slept less and ate little. Richard's thoughts lived alone in a place of utter darkness. Hobbys gave him some herbs such that he slept more, but Richard found difficulty on concentrating clearly on affairs of state until after Matins.

How strange, thought Hobbys, the King is the foremost citizen of England, a role to which all would aspire, some with royal blood and perhaps a realistic claim as an heir to the throne, some menial serfs who would remain at the bottom of life's pyramid till the day they died. Yet they would all leap at the idea of being king for a day. In reality it was a lonely position, and none lonelier than Richard. Most had a wife who would see the king in private moments as a mortal man, with all the strengths and frailties of an ordinary man, someone who could offer succour as no one else could. Richard had nobody, though God's anointed king, he experienced a loneliness deeper than anyone should. Hobbys filled the role of private confidant. He could show his physician anxieties and weaknesses he could not reveal to his closest friends amongst the martial men who surround a king, they looked only for strength and leadership. Hobbys thought it strange that he should feel so sorry for a king.

# HOLBORN JUNE 1485

Hammering on Hobbys door again presaged some disaster. A dusty, sweaty soldier, again bearing the royal coat of arms stood at the door. 'Pack your bags, get your equipment, and saddle up your horse, Master Hobbys, the king has need of you now. He has moved to Nottingham ready to defend our kingdom against the Tudor who is expected to invade any day.'

Hobbys made his way on his cart with all his medical supplies and his two apprentices. Two weeks travel saw him arrive at Nottingham castle. He had mixed feelings about the impending battle. Many of Richard's former allies had deserted him believing that he may have murdered his nephews. Poor Richard was unable to tell the truth of the unfortunate boys, and Hobbys was reminded occasionally of his oath of secrecy. If Richard informed the world that Edward V had died of natural causes, few would believe him. This may be the last battle, a good event for the kingdom, but battles were a rich source of bodies for his research. He hoped to work out why some dead bodies had empty hearts and great vessels on death and some did not, it was a bizarre problem

# LEICESTER AUGUST 19TH 1485

Hobbys drew up his wagon of medical supplies by Bow Bridge on the road out of Leicester, waiting for Richard's army to pass by. He could hear the noise of trumpeters and drummers coming from the middle of the city. Soon they appeared leading the massive army, their instruments and tabards emblazoned with the leopards and lilies of the king, and the white boar of Gloucester. Next in the van came the foot soldiers and archers of Norfolk and his son Surrey with a cavalry screen on either side, behind them were Richard and his great nobles, Norfolk, Surrey and Northumberland, Lord Zouche and William Berkeley, the Earl of Nottingham. The king was in full armour, his gold crown on his head, and the banners of England and St George fluttering over his head. It was an awesome sight. Finally the Duke of Northumberland's troop brought up the rear. The army of thousands with shining armour, lances and swords, with royal standards fluttering in the breeze looked invincible.

However; an unpleasant incident struck a chilling feeling into the panoply of majesty, as Richard rode over the bridge, his spurs caught some stones with a clash of sparks. The old witch of Leicester, a reputed soothsayer, wailed that Richard's head would strike the same spot in a few days when his corpse was carried back into town after his defeat on the field of battle. Norfolk laughed and pushed her aside, but transient glances of apprehension were visible on the faces of all who knew and heard her.

Once the soldiers had passed, Hobbys swung his wagon into line ahead of the baggage train, forcing the leading wagon to break abruptly, accompanied by some foul curses from the two wagon drivers in the front. Clearly Hobbys thought, they did not understand that the royal physician and the medical supplies wagon was the next most important part of an army on the march after the king's soldiers.

# BOSWORTH FIELD AUGUST 21ˢᵀ 1485

Hobbys followed Richard's army from Leicester driving his wagon of medical supplies. Hobbys was ordered once the battlefield was reached to erect his tent for casualties just below the top of the hill out of sight of the Tudor's oncoming forces. As sergeant surgeon, he would be responsible for treating any wounds that the king may suffer, but it seemed more likely that either Richard or the Tudor would be beyond any skills Hobbys may have by the end of the battle.

After sunset, Hobbys was summoned to the royal tent where Richard and his immediate close supporting knights were checking their armour.

'Hobbys,' called the king, 'This man here is Lord Strange, one of Stanley's sons. He has come here to ensure the battle against the Tudor goes well, and to remind Thomas of his loyalty to England. Thomas Stanley keeps his honour in a container somewhat like a dovecote, with few worthy contents, most compartments contain only excreta. A man is defined by the honour of his companions not by his titles. Tudor, or Richmond by the title he claims, is defined by his friendship with treacherous scum like Stanley. As your king, I am defined by men such as Norfolk, as loyal and courageous a man as you will find in all England,' he said slapping the Duke on the back. Turning back to Hobbys, he said, 'Should Stanley fail to respond to my orders, you may have this body for your dissection; just chop his head off before you start, though that probably does not matter, perhaps you could chop his head off after you have finished. I expect you will find he is gutless, heartless and has a lily liver like his father.'

Then Hobbys replied, 'thank you your grace, that will be an interesting experience, I am curious to see if there is any difference in the hearts of nobles and peasants.' Strange went pale and sagged at the knees briefly before regaining his composure. He remained silent recognising that words would be useless. 'And Hobbys,' continued the King, 'your loyalty to the House of York has always been appreciated, better than that pompous schemer, Argentine, he seems the medical equivalent of Stanley, always out to inflate his importance and his purse. He ran off to the Tudor, or Italy somewhere, and has been spreading foul rumours for a year or more that the princes have been murdered. He told the Italian writer Mancini that story, Mancini is some Italian traveller who can't speak English, has never met me and left England in July 1483, and he has also been writing these foul lies, at least you know the truth. Should anything go wrong tomorrow you will be my most important witness that I loved my father, brothers, son and nephews, that I would not harm a hair of their heads, be sure to let the world know. Should all go well England will be able to think of crusading again, our Lord must be expecting us to turn back the Turks and retake our Holy Land".

After a brief silence Richard continued, 'Hobbys, you enjoy quoting Socrates, perhaps you recall him saying *death may be the greatest of all human blessings.*'

The cool autumn breeze moaned softly through the trees, then suddenly a gust of wind blew open the back canvas flap of the Royal Pavilion. Richard started and pulled his dagger, though no one came in, nobody visible that was, but some flickering insubstantial thing brushed past Hobbys and the King like a ghost in the air. Strangely pictures came to Hobbys of deaths on the battlefield, pictures in his mind of Harold on the Senlac Ridge with an arrow in his eye, and the Dukes of York and Rutland at Wakefield.

Outside in the night sky the moon with all its pits and markings shone with a green colour through the late summer humidity, looking for all the world like a skull. It would be either Tudor's or Richard's at the end of tomorrow. Should Richard win it would confirm his right to the English throne by his royal blood and his courage in adversity, it would also be the Tower for those not committed to his side. It was a scene where something was about to end, and the start of something new, only God knew who would wear the crown on the morrow.

As Hobbys walked back to his tent, he could hear whispers all round him. The words were inaudible, but there was a subliminal atmosphere of treachery and shifting allegiances in the darkness. Hobbys feared for the king's future on the 'morrow. With second thoughts, he feared for himself, it could be one of those moments in life when everything he had built for himself crumbled to dust. Having been an eminent physician to the Yorkist family for a quarter of a century, he would not expect any favours from the Tudors, especially when he was aware that Margaret may have poisoned King Edward.

Hobbys realised he had never discussed the incident with the foxgloves with anyone before. He turned on his heel and walked back to the king's tent wondering how to introduce the subject. However; on peering through rear flap of the king's pavilion he saw Richard alone on his knees before a crucifix, his words just audible as he read from his book of hours, 'Lord Jesus Christ, deign to free me, your servant King Richard, from every tribulation, sorrow and trouble in which I am placed. Hear me in the name of all your goodness, for which I give thanks........' Hobbys crept silently away, like Richard to sleep fitfully, the one having nightmares about his future, the other having nightmares about the past.

# AUGUST 22ND 1485

On the morning of the battle, the king's men rose at first light to hear mass. Hobbys knelt before the priest but felt he would not need to make a full confession of his past sins as the battle should not last too long before the Tudor's head was on a spike, and Hobbys was unlikely to face death, or even be severely wounded. He was dimly aware of Richard's chaplain droning on, 'Show me and pour over me your grace and glory....' His monotonous voice took Hobbys back to the French campaign, which came to nothing apart from many such prayers and some unique pleasures, which distracted Hobbys for a few moments, but the chaplain was still going, 'therefore Lord Jesus Christ, son of the living God, deign to free me, thy servant King Richard...' A few more minutes and the sacrament for Richard and his closest associates before the mass ended.

After mass, Sir William Catesby came galloping up the hill to the king's tent, leapt off his horse and fell on one knee in front of Richard. Looking up at Richard he said 'He refuses sire.'

'Come on man, get up and tell me exactly what he said.' responded Richard.

'My lord, I went to the bastard Tudor's tent under a flag of truce as you ordered, though they drew swords and threatened me. I told the cowardly Tudor that you offered mortal combat, man to man, knight to knight, one to one to settle the throne once and for ever, and to spare innocent lives on the battle field.' answered Catesby.

'Yes, and how did the Tudor reply, answer me with his exact words?' demanded Richard.

'My Lord the Tudor went pale and silent, but after a few moments Jasper Tudor spoke out. 'My Lord Catesby,' he said, 'God's chosen king would not fight a deformed usurper, a berserker. The battle will be settled by the time hallowed battlefield generalship, and by strategic alliances.' Catesby paused, 'My Lord, when Jasper said strategic alliances, all his followers laughed. My Lord, be sure that your trust in your allies is merited.' Said Catesby looking at Lord Strange and then at Northumberland.

Richard looked thoughtfully at Northumberland. 'The Tudor may find his cowardly soul tested today, his mother has more courage in her little finger than he in his whole body. Let the battle begin.'

Catesby said, "Back to your tent Hobbys, there will be hot work for you and us, though hopefully most of your casualties will be misguided souls from the bastard Tudor's camp.'

As Hobbys reluctantly walked back down the slope, he could hear the call to arms, trumpets sounding the advance, the thump of marching men's' feet, the shouts of derision as Tudor's vanguard approached sooner than expected. Soon bloodied and dying men with severed limbs and horrendous injuries to the trunk began to flow into Hobbys tent. Amputations, suturing and plentiful laudanum filled the next half hour for Hobbys, when a shout went up that Jockey of Norfolk was down.

Hobbys walked briefly up the hill to discover how the battle was progressing and to get an idea of how many more casualties he should expect. He saw Norfolk's men falling back before Oxford's onslaught, Northumberland standing beside his horse to the rear, apparently having declined Richard's order to reinforce Norfolk, and Richard pointing out the Tudor's position to the right and behind his troops.

Hobbys thought Richard would be wondering what Edward would have done in this predicament. Choices for this battlefield chess board were reducing rapidly, Richard's Queen had died last year, one of his castles, Norfolk, had just fallen in the front of the battle line, the ranks of death, the other, Northumberland, has refused to advance his pawns. Hobbys thought the hottest places in hell should be reserved for such cowards trying to be neutral on a battlefield. Bishops were little use one fighting started. All that left was the king and his knights!

Hobbys heard Richard shout. "There is the Tudor, skulking like the coward he is behind his troops, let us end this man to man, he will find out glittering ranks are made of steel as well as gold, cold steel for a false pretender. I will live or die as a Plantagenet King of England, CAVALRY CHARGE, knights of the body to me!"

Richard's Knights and esquires of his body, Francis Lovell, Ratcliffe and Brackenbury to the fore, followed by James Harrington, Marmaduke Constable, Thomas Burgh, Ralph Assheton, Thomas Pilkington, John Sapcote, and the Staffords, Thomas and Hugh all leapt into their saddles. Men of proven loyalty and courage. A magnificent sight of shining armour and lethal weapons, but not as many men as William Stanley's cavalry just watching menacingly but motionless to the side.

With that Richard took off down the hill on his white charger, Blanc Sanglier, Ratcliffe and Brackenbury beside him, Catesby just behind and some two hundred knights hurtled down the hill to the right of the clash of foot soldiers. The pennants of the white boar and leopards of England flew out above them, a magnificent and terrifying sight. Hobbys thought that here was his chance to show his metal, that he could use a broadsword as well as his favoured rapier, that he could be there as Richard slew the Tudor, or preferably immediately after when the enemy army was leaderless, disencouraged and about to surrender, and then enjoy the glory his shares of the spoils of battle. He leaped on his horse, ordered Strange to remain there, and set off in pursuit, but he became aware out of the corner of his eye a mass movement to his right, it was William Stanley's cavalry, at least a thousand of them charging, Hobbys hoped to help Richard destroy the Tudor, "Oh my God, NO, Sire beware!" he yelled in vain over the din of battle, they were charging at Richard. Hobbys veered a bit to the left, glory seemed a little less assured.

Elizabeth Wydville's comments back ten years ago, before the French campaign about Richard not enjoying a cavalry charge, came back to Hobbys, that women has an eerie ability to see the future.

The king at the front of his knights had slain one huge man, possible Henry's bodyguard William Brandon with a clean battle-axe strike through his neck, Ouch, and then unhorsed another even taller knight possible Sir Henry Cheney as Hobbys peered through the dust at their colours. The Tudor could be seen ducked down behind some French pikemen only a few feet from Richard. Then Stanley's troop crashed into the flank of Richard's men who began falling like nine pins, outnumbered, outflanked and betrayed. Hobbys saw Richard still wearing his helmet and crown unhorsed, then sink beneath a hoard of attackers, still holding of two men in front of him, but downed by massive blows to the head from behind which dislodged his helmet and smashed into the back of his head.

Hobbys slowed his horse, then became aware of the other Stanley, Lord Thomas approaching from his left. Glory had evaporated; he turned his horse around and galloped off the battlefield aware of distant pursuit which he evaded through the wood nearby. He returned hastily to Westminster Palace, changing his horse once near Northampton, ahead of the disastrous news, collected his medical equipment and his precious library of ancient venerable texts, before taking refuge in his rooms in London, planning to deny any significant involvement in the battle. Hobbys would not be able to assist in the funeral rites of Richard as he had for Edward.

Nor could he, the most eminent physician to the Yorkist family for a quarter of a century, anticipate any benefits from the Henry Tudor, or his mother, especially with his knowledge of Margaret bringing foxgloves into the palace and perhaps poisoning King Edward, and now that the Tudor was too great a coward to face the king in battle after Catesby's morning embassy to the enemy camp.

Days later Hobbys heard the story going around London that the king's naked body had been despoiled in death with his buttocks being stabbed while his corpse with a rope around his neck was draped over the back of a horse. On the return trip to Leicester, Richard's head did strike Bow Bridge as the old hag had predicted. His body was exposed naked in Leicester for all to see he was dead, then his corpse was buried in a hastily dug grave in the choir of Grey Friars Church. Apparently the grave was not long enough for his body, he was tossed in with his hands tied, with no embalming, no shroud and no ceremony. Henry Tudor in his moment of triumph had revealed his base character, his lack of chivalry, Richard would never have treated the body of an adversary in battle like this.

# WESTMINSTER PLACE SEPTEMBER 1ST 1485

Henry lounged casually on his throne, his thin lips perpetually turned down. No trace of terror remained on his bony face, though in his darkest dreams he could not forget the unrestrained ferocity on Richard's face as he wielded his battle-axe brutally, skilfully, through William Brandon's neck, before being struck down from behind with a halberd only a few paces away. Sometimes he wondered privately who was the usurper, but a smile from his mother, the only other person in the room, standing beside the throne in her new favourite position reassured him of his divine right to be sitting there. Margaret as always was positioned on the moral high ground and swathed in her armour of self-righteousness. Currently it glowed in victory and vindication as she basked in her title as 'My Lady, the King's Mother.' In the past it had glowered with bitterness, a bitterness built from scraps of information about those who had failed to appreciate her son's God-given right to the throne of England, about those who had belittled the Tudors as insignificant members of the nobility. In triumph, she would not forget the tittle-tattle; magnanimity was not part of her make-up.

Henry and Margaret Beaufort were conducting private interviews, seeking information, vital closet information, secrets to he harboured till the right moment, priceless scandals, treasonous whispers, facts to be used to ensure their domination of England, facts to be used against the nobility should they stray out of line, facts which could be extracted painlessly here, or painfully in the Tower, it mattered little. Mostly they needed to know what had happened to Edward's sons, they could hardly proclaim Elizabeth of York to be the rightful queen if the boys were still alive. Their guards were nearby and all their supporters and nobility dismissed to encourage the release of secret information in confidence.

Hobbys was marched into the palace between four stony-faced guards. Not a word was said. No inkling of what was to happen was divulged. The possibility of immediate execution like poor Catesby suffered tested Hobbys sphincters almost beyond control. Reaching an outer chamber a bench was indicated to him where he sat fingering the cross around his neck. While he hadn't exactly followed all the teachings of our lord, he hoped for some support and forgiveness at this late and critical stage. The guards watched suspiciously across the room. Faint conversation just reached his ears from behind the arras.

'We must be sure,' hissed a voice sounding like Margaret Beaufort. Hobbys heard Henry call 'next,' and Margaret, now addressed by all at her insistence as Margaret, lady mother to the king, said, 'These next two knaves bring details from the tower of Edward's sons.' Two men entered reluctantly, fingering their caps and falling to their knees in front of the throne.

'So fools what news do you bring me,' said Henry haughtily.

A tremulous voice was just heard by Hobbys from beyond the curtain, 'your majesty, we crave your indulgence, we tried to follow your orders, forgive us our mistake.'

Henry cut in angrily, 'idiots, did you not carry out my orders?'

'Your majesty, we found two children dressed as princes high in the attic of the white tower, we smothered them so no trace of violence could be seen, and buried them in the darkness outside the white tower so no one saw us, but your majesty, when we stripped the bodies of all identification as you ordered we found them to be girls!'

Margaret and Henry gasped in shock. Margaret as usual, after a life time of quick thinking under pressure, gathered her wits together first.

'Girls, you imbeciles, you oafs, GUARDS, GUARDS,' cried Margaret, grasping the sword beside Henry's throne and reflecting that she could probably use it more effectively than her son.

A rush of pounding feet made Hobbys leap to his feet, and look back at the exit while his guards looked up at him menacingly. He sat down again, to hear Margaret's hysterical voice shout, 'Gag these men at once, let them say not another word, take them out and execute them immediately, off with their heads.' Noises of cries and a brief scuffle followed, then silence fell. He could hear a few whispers from the Tudor mother and son, but could not hear what was said. A brief pregnant pause followed.

'Next!' called Henry. Hobbys entered hesitantly when his guards gestured to him with their halberds. He approached the throne reluctantly and sank to his knees looking at Henry's feet. The king surveyed the man kneeling in front of him distastefully.

'So Master Hobbys, did you hear our discussion with the last gentlemen here?'

Hobbys thinking quickly said, 'I am sorry your majesty, my hearing has been damaged by too many battlefield cannons, could you repeat your question?'

Henry and Margaret looked at each other, then the king continued, 'Hobbys, you have the misfortune to have been a faithful servant of the House of York, even the child killer, the usurping Richard, that foul blots on God's blessed kingdom.' Henry's French accentuated speech and long wavy hair below his shoulders in the European fashion betrayed the many years he had spent out of England. Margaret Beaufort clutched the Middleham Jewel suspended from the gold chain around her neck, marvelling at her family's rise to power, and the fall of the house of York since one of her spies in Middleham Castle had stolen it four years ago. Margaret reflected that she was clearly a much more worthy person in the eyes of the Lord, and that this was a natural reward for her piety and faith.

Hobbys looking up noted with astonishment Margaret's religious icon, the blue sapphire above the gold crucifixion scene that had been King Richard's Middleham Jewel, of all people in England Margaret Beaufort would be the most likely person to have 'found' it. Margaret hissed at Hobbys, 'fool, what are you gawping at?'

Hobbys stammered, 'Your grace, your icon, it once belonged to the late Queen Anne.'

'Yes, fool, before her household donated it to us, it belonged to the most unfortunate Anne Neville, now at the rest she deserves. She once was the beautiful happy wife of Edward of Lancaster, that white knight, that flower of Christendom, cruelly cut down after Tewksbury by the foul usurper. The unfortunate Anne was then abducted and forced into marriage with the murderer of children. No wonder God moved to ensure his seed should not survive in this land. So, who more appropriate to receive an image of the crucifixion of our Lord, we who are blessed by God, whose love and bounty now rightly shines on the house of Tudor.'

Henry fidgeted uncomfortably at Margaret's egregious piety, wishing she could sometimes reduce the incessant flow of greater godliness than all other mortals. Margaret was looking at her son with unadulterated pride, he was the centre of her universe, the sole star in her heaven. For decades she had circled protectively around him, a stealthy moon, silently, mercilessly, mostly unobserved, and eliminating those who may eclipse his brilliance. Her dogged determination, her unfailing ruthless pursuit of his negligible claim to the throne had effectively brought an adventurer of minor nobility to the highest throne of the land. Hobbys banished his disbelief in favour of extreme humility, a preferred policy of survival when so many of greater importance than he had been eliminated from the royal court.

'Your Majesty, I have been a true and faithful servant of all those who have entrusted me with their care regardless of their status and allegiance,' Hobbys glanced up at the high cheek bones, and narrowed eyes looking menacingly at him.

'Yet not so competent when three kings die on your watch in a couple of years, as well as the old Duke of York and the young Edmund, Earl of Rutland before that,' replied the king.

Margaret Beaufort in her usual spiteful manner said, 'we will not require your services much longer when there are clearly wiser and more competent doctors around. You will not receive any further pay or pension from the royal coffers. I think we should retain the services of Master John Argentine as Royal Physician, he has a more eminent status amongst his colleagues than you master Hobbys, he certainly seems more knowledgeable and competent. His important patients don't all die!'

Hobbys seethed inwardly, then whined, 'Your majesty, I am but God's servant, his will is immeasurably greater than my poor clinical skills.'

Margaret continued, 'We shall also retain the services of Lewis Caerleon. A most competent sensitive doctor with much more awareness of changing times and who would rule the future than yourself.'

Hobbys boiled again in silence. Caerleon was a doctor of astronomy not medicine. Caerleon apparently still followed the doctrine of John Mirfield, a priest and physician at St Bartholomew's Hospital nearly 100 years ago. Mirfield believed that a doctor should add the number of letters of the patient's name, the referring messenger's name and the day of the week to ascertain the outcome. If the resulting sum was an even number the unfortunate person would die, if it were an odd number recovery would occur. Fancy having a physician who still believed such rubbish. Caerleon had also been a secret agent pretending to be a physician while communicating covertly between Margaret and

Elizabeth Woodville to arrange the marriage of Elizabeth, a Princess of York, with the Tudor. A marriage with a commoner would at least have been to a legitimate citizen rather than a bastard line. No wonder Richard had Caerleon imprisoned in the Tower for being a traitor! As for seeing the future, Caerleon have once provided old Henry VI a horoscope, that was now hushed up having been wrong in almost all its predictions, mind you, he thought, even the greatest pessimist, not one given the task of predicting a glorious future, would have guessed what a disaster that poor old man would become.

'Yes My lady,' Hobbys muttered.

'Yet you seem to have accumulated considerable wealth from you private practice charging exorbitant fees as the royal physician,' said Margaret. Hobbys remained silent; this was a difficult charge to deny he thought as many patients had quite reasonably reviewed his skilled compassionate care with appropriate benevolence.

'So, Master Hobbys,' Margaret continued, 'we gather from Lord Strange that you were at Bosworth.'

Hobbys could see that he had to admit that. 'Yes your majesty, on the orders of the last king, but I fled from his army as soon as possible. King Richard ordered me to slay Lord Strange, but that would be against my Hippocratic Oath, how could I kill a defenceless young man, so I spared his life.' whined Hobbys hopefully.

'Master Hobbys, can you tell me where Viscount Lovell may be hiding?' asked Margaret. 'No Madam, his whereabouts is a mystery to all,' replied Hobbys.

 Next Margaret asked, 'Tell us about the usurper's bent body and mind, what deformities did you find?'

'My lady, King Richard was short but strong in limb and mind, notwithstanding the debateable way of how he came to the throne, he died a warrior's death.' Henry winced transiently at the memory.

Margaret continued, 'so master Hobbys, were you acquainted with the King Edward's harlot, Mistress Shore?'

Hobbys tried to compose himself, surely no one else was aware of his brief dalliance, and Jane had not yet been found. 'Your Majesty, I saw her on my occasional visits to the court, but her health was such that she never needed my professional services,' more the other way round Hobbys reflected transiently.

'Idiot! Margaret hissed, 'Did you ever bed her?'

'Oh,' inhaled Hobbys in shock, wondering what punishment he may suffer for their one dalliance. He needed to claim distance from the royal court in all aspects. 'Lady Mother to the King!' Hobbys hoped he has the right title to flatter her status. 'Jane Shore was the King's mistress; any such relationship would have been lèse-majesté and more than my life would have been worth, also as physician to the king, I take my ethical obligations very seriously, and equally I have been faithfully married with three children for many years, I would not dream of such a wicked thing,' he tried pompously. Though he did dream of it often afterwards, God she was beautiful, and skilled in bed. 'Er, well I was married.'

'And Master Hobbys, we know about your divorce,' continued Margaret, 'Do you have any idea why King Edward died?'

She looked intently into Hobbys eyes, could she have seen him watching when she entered the palace carrying foxgloves, he thought not. 'Your ladyship, I believe he caught a chill while fishing,' he responded.

Margaret continued her questioning, 'Hobbys, were you in the usurper's tent on the morning of the battle?' She must wonder if Hobbys was the only survivor with Yorkist sympathies to know of the Tudor's cowardice when challenged to mortal combat. Lord Strange would have known he was there. 'Your ladyship, I was there briefly before the battle commenced, but having received my instructions, I returned to my tent to await the arrival of wounded soldiers.'

'Hobbys, did you see the traitor Catesby talk to the usurper?' persisted Margaret. 'Yes your ladyship, they spoke often, but discreetly. I was not privy to any of their conversations. I have only a humble…'

'Yes, yes, we are tired of hearing about your false humility,' interrupted Margaret. Apparently convinced Henry continued Hobbys interrogation.

'Master Hobbys, you were a frequent confidant of the late foul usurper, tell us of your visits to Edward V, and his young brother, the Duke of York in the Tower?'

'Your majesty, I was but the humble physician to King Edward, and his brother King Richard, I was not privy to information beyond that of their health. Mine was a lowly position in the palace, I was only summoned in the event of sickness, and indeed I had to be guided to your throne room. As you stated, Dr Argentine was the most eminent physician in the land, and he cared for the young princes,' Hobbys hoped his face did not give him away; years of lying to his patients should stand him in good stead.

'I saw Prince Edward before he went to Ludlow with the Earl of Rivers, and saw Prince Richard up to the time of King Edward's death, but his mother, your betrothed's mother, withdrew him into sanctuary, and I never saw either again,' lied Hobbes fluently. Ratcliffe, Catesby, Richard, Stafford and Brackenbury were all dead; hopefully there were no survivors aware of his deceit.

'Your majesty, I have always kept records of my treatment of all my patients. They are secreted safely where none can find them, but I can show you copies of any you wish to see. Obviously they are subject to professional confidentiality, and I would request your majesty that they are treated discretely.' Hobbys would have time to doctor his records and only present those he was prepared to show the Tudor. 'I would be pleased to show you that I am learned in the arts of medicine and have followed closely the teachings of our medical forefathers, Hippocrates and Avicenna are…'

'Shut up you stupid fool,' hissed Margaret.

Henry and Margaret looked at him suspiciously. Margaret whispered in Henry's ear, 'I never met such a humble royal physician before. Perhaps a visit to the tower may aid his memory.'

'No your majesty, no!' grovelled Hobbys as his bladder sphincter gave up the unequal struggle. 'I have only been a humble, very humble doctor; I know only professional confidences of minimal importance. From today I will serve you truly, and any of your nobles as required, let me be your informant from this day.'

The Tudor thought for a while, peering into Hobbys innermost thought. 'Well Master Hobbys, we will spare your miserable existence, we have two tasks left for you which will spare your life for the moment, firstly you will inform our secretary of any Yorkist plots, the merest whispers you hear from your previous confidants against our throne, the whereabouts of Lovell should you hear any rumours, and secondly, having been her physician in previous years, you will examine our betrothed, Elizabeth of York, we will send her to her rooms where you will await her arrival, to ensure she has all the traits of fertility so we can establish the Tudor dynasty. Dr Argentine has not yet arrived back from France, but childbearing is not one of his many skills. Then remove yourself and your stinking trousers from this court, and never show your face in London or my presence again unless you have information for me. Should we find you have lied to us you will experience a visit to the tower to the rack and branding iron, before being hung, castrated, drawn and quartered, do we make ourselves clear"

Margaret Beaufort whispered in Henry's ear, 'My son, I think he tells the truth, he was of little importance, Argentine was so much more skilled than he, we should keep him alive, perhaps he could lead us to Francis Lovell, wherever he may be skulking, or even, with his record of deaths, care for John, my Lord of Lincoln, once heir to the foul usurper,' Henry Tudor laughed. William Hobbys, physician to the three Yorkist kings, bowed to the throne and backed out hastily, while thinking to himself, how typical of Argentine to await the outcome of Bosworth and then choose the winning side, and no, anything practical in the way of basic bodily functions was not Argentine's forte.

Hobbys brushed the arras aside and sat down on a bench perspiring heavily, his shirt as wet as his trousers. He had feared execution like poor Catesby after the battle, or perhaps as a commoner, the frightful ordeal of strangling, castration, disembowelment and beheading. He hastened out of the Palace, washed and changed in the adjacent tavern and re-entered the palace to await Elizabeth of York, reflecting that he would spend the remainder of his days secreted in the cloisters of his college back in Oxford, translating the works of Avicenna into modern English adding comments from his own experiences. Only he, Henry Tudor and Henry's mother now knew of the substitution of the princes in the tower, and only he knew of what had happened to them.

# WESTMINSTER PLACE SEPTEMBER 2ND 1485

Hobbys sat outside the bedchamber for half an hour waiting till Tudor's espoused wife was sent to her quarters. When summoned Hobbys entered the bedchamber of Elizabeth of York diffidently, wearing his best clothing, all dry and unstained. Elizabeth lay on her bed, a sheet drawn up around her neck, her ladies-in-waiting seated across the room. He did not recognise any of them, he suspected they had all been replaced with Henry's choices, or more likely those of the new she-wolf, Margaret Beaufort, a lady with all the attributes of stealth, ruthlessness, secrecy and merciless determination for her son that the last Margaret, the one of Anjou displayed and some more on top. Beaufort, against all the odds, and a bastard line or two, had been successful.

'Your Grace, I am aware from our previous meeting that you have enjoyed excellent health since your early childhood,' Hobbys croaked hoarsely, 'however the king, your betrothed, has asked me to ensure your health and fertility before your marriage, so I must ask some personal questions. Can you tell me are your monthly bleedings, your moon blood, regular and normal, do you have any pain or discharge?'

'Master Hobbys, I can assure you they are quite satisfactory from a male perspective.' responded Elizabeth.

'Your grace,' whispered Hobbys, 'please excuse the question but I must ask. Can you tell me if you have ever known a man, if so was it a painful experience and have you ever conceived?'

'Master Hobbys, what a question,' Elizabeth whispered back obliquely, 'I have never known a living man, so how can I say if it would have hurt, or if I have ever conceived.'

Hobbys recognised an evasive answer after more than twenty years of experiencing patients telling less than the truth, he was left wondering like many in Richard III's court if she may have known a man no longer living.'

'However, Master Hobbys, you may examine me,' she said suddenly throwing the sheet off to reveal her totally naked body underneath. Oh God, though Hobbys, she is as beautiful as Mistress Jane, more beautiful than her mother, Elizabeth Woodville, as he struggled to keep his thoughts on a professional level, did Henry realise what a fortunate man he was?

Elisabeth looked him in the eye, and said coquettishly, 'Mistress Jane told me you had all the skills to make an expert accoucheur Master Hobbes!'

Hobbys dropped his medical bag in panic, Oh God, she knew, 'my life will be forfeit in agony should the king believe any unprofessional rumours about me, your grace,' he begged.

'Your secrets are safe with me Hobbys, as I trust mine are with you, proceed.' she responded, and extended her arm to Hobbys, her fist closed tightly around something. She turned her hand over and opened it to reveal a gold icon, with a blue sapphire set above a crucifixion scene, 'will you return this to Middleham for me in memory of my late uncle?'

'Your grace, we understand each other excellently.' Hobbys, totally astonished, whispered gratefully, hiding the jewel below his robes.

Hobbys was overcome with anxiety, confusion and yes lust, he needed to listen to her heart and chest, but did not trust himself to lay his ear on her gorgeous breasts without experiencing problems which could become visible to others in the room. An inspiration came to him, he rolled up a sheet of his notes, and placed one end delicately on the middle of her chest, between her breasts and listened to the other, Goodness! Her heart sounds could be heard very clearly, he moved the tube to the left of her chest just under the breast taking care not to touch it as Elizabeth watched in amusement. Again he could clearly hear her heart sounds, they were reassuringly normal, and significantly slower than his. What a discovery, he could present that to the college, a Hobscope, his name would be remembered forever in medical circles.

He finished his examination rapidly, carefully. He wished she had not moaned quietly but provocatively when he examined her vaginal introitus, while still looking straight into his eyes. She was deliberately trying and succeeding to distract him for her own amusement.

Elizabeth grimaced briefly and said, 'I suppose I have no option but to go through this marriage with the Tudor? I will have to see it as my duty to my father's kingdom, I shall just close my eyes, lie on my back and think of England.'

Elizabeth's face suddenly went blank and her eyes peered into the remote distance and she said softly, mystically, 'my second son will charter a royal college of physicians that you have sought so long when Thomas returns from the Holy City.' Hobbys was confused by this prophecy. Why her second son, who was Thomas, it did not make sense.

He found everything in her physical health to be normal, stammered his reassurances and congratulations and left the room to find Margaret Beaufort standing in the corridor awaiting him. 'No lies this time, Master Hobbys,' she hissed, 'is she a virgin, will she be fertile?'

'My lady, the king's mother,' Hobbys stammered again, feeling his bladder sphincter loosening a little, 'yes and yes, Elizabeth of York is intact and in excellent health, and I am sure she will bear the king many sons. My records of Princess Elizabeth show her to have had excellent health all her life in spite of the traumas around her.'

Margaret smiled victoriously. Hobbys was getting really irritated as well as terrified by Margaret's superior attitude, he thought he may seek some revenge when the Tudor was not present. 'My lady, mother to the king, my records are very comprehensive, but hidden where only I can find them. They note that Stillington only informed King Richard about King Edward's earlier betrothal at your suggestion giving Richard no option but to take the throne. They even record your preference of flowers, the red rose first and the foxglove second.'

Margaret was struck dumb, she went very pale. Richard may have confided in Hobbys more than he admitted. Even now Edward had been dead for over two years, a court case by the peers of the realm for the poisoning of a king, a God's anointed king could go badly against her. She could have ordered Hobbys execution with a click of her fingers, but secret records might emerge latter.

'Master Hobbys,' she seethed, regaining her composure, 'Anything you say against the king's grace will result in your secret places being discovered by the experts in the Tower, be aware they are as good at their job as you may be at yours. Like you they understand how much pain the body can tolerate without dying, but unlike you they have no use for laudanum, do I make myself clear?'

'Thank you your grace, perfectly clear, and I will definitely let you know if any rumours about Lovell or treasonous plots reach my ears.'

Hobbys left the palace as fast as possible after packing all his books and equipment and mounting his horse, thank God the horse could not speak, rode rapidly out of London.

# OCTOBER 30TH, 1485

The Tudor was crowned on this day. Hobbys was not surprised that he was not invited, though apparently Argentine and Caerleon were. Hobbys was amused to be given copies of the public program after the event. It was the same document used for Richard's coronation with his name crossed out and replaced by the Tudor's. Was this because Henry was the miser as rumoured, already saving money for the royal coffers or just unprepared. At least the crowd of spectators had written instructions of when to cheer for King Henry!

# JANUARY 1486

Hobbys went back to the Middlesex Hospital on a foggy winter's day, carefully cloaked and hooded, in early 1486 to make enquiries. The mother superior perused the records of 1483. 'Yes, we admitted a Ned Broome to the leprosarium in June 1483, accompanied by a Dr Hobbys,' she looked up, 'You!'

'Funny, you are the second person to make enquiries about patients admitted here late in 1483; a clerk wearing Tudor livery was going round all the London hospitals a couple of months ago trying to find records of anything. I told him we kept no records, fancy thinking I would help some bloody Tudor's lackey, excuse my un-convent like language doctor.'

'He deteriorated fairly rapidly and died in early 1484. The leprosy seemed to affect his mind and he became very confused. From when he began to deteriorate right up to the end he demanded that the staff should call him your majesty, and go down on bended knee to kiss his ring. His last words were something like 'God bless Richard'. He had what looked like a very expensive but small ring, gold with a ruby set into it, when he died, the ring disappeared from his body. He was buried somewhere in an unmarked grave under an oak tree within sight of St Paul's Cathedral on Hampstead Hill at night, as is our policy so no one sees us.'

The shrewd old nun looked carefully at Hobbys. 'We never knew who he really was, I don't think he really was Ned Broome, he never seemed to answer to that name. However I have my own ideas, I think you know who he was, but you are not about to tell me are you?'

'You may be correct,' said Hobbys, 'but I couldn't possibly comment.'

'Hm,' said the mother superior, watching Hobbys face vigilantly for clues, 'We buried him wrapped in an old Yorkist battle flag and the Royal Standard of Edward IV just in case his ramblings were correct.'

'A nice touch, thank you mother Superior,' replied Hobbys with not a flicker of emotion

# THE TEMPLE CHURCH, HOLBORN AUGUST 1488

'**M**aster Hobbys, it is indeed a very long confession, and not before time, as you expect to meet your maker soon. I don't think it will make a big difference if you are unable to remember all the ladies names or places. I do not think God will be interested in the various positions or other intimate details which you seem able to recall rather easily and wistfully. I do think it will shorten your time in purgatory, should you make significant bequests to the church to pray for your soul. I suggest you meet with your lawyer soon to make some generous amendments to your will.'

Hobbys, again on his knees looked anxiously at the priest. 'I have dedicated my life to the welfare of my patients, with little thought for my own safety or status, and little concern for my income above the need to cure my patients. I had hope that God would perhaps look kindly on the good aspects of my life, and forgive the er, peccadilloes. Would a few Hail Mary's be of benefit as well?' he said optimistically.

# HOLBORN 15ᵀᴴ AUGUST 1488

'**W**elcome, sir, Master Hobbys, it is always a pleasure to see you.' ingratiated his lawyer, 'how may I help you today?'

'I fear the grim reaper, who has collected so many of my patients is about to come for me, and I need to finalise my will,' replied Hobbys.

'I nominate my daughters Agnes and Mercy to act as my executors and I will read you my list of beneficiaries.'

Hobbys continued, 'To John Stavely, surgeon and my son-in-law I leave all my medical texts and equipment. I forgive him for destroying my marriage, he was obliged to state what he thought he saw. To my grandson and medical student William Stavely my favourite book Compendium Qui Adiscit de Arto Generali. To John Northorne, my surgical apprentice I leave my mixing bowl and pot, and all the expert teaching he has received from me.

I wish to recognise the importance of my professional guilds for their assistance in my prominent career. I leave the ornate silver cup and five pounds to the Masters and Wardens barber-surgeons of London to pay for a communal dinner for 'both men and women' and for prayers to be said for Alice and myself annually. I leave 6s 8p to the master, wardens & brothers of my art of surgeon to pay for food and drink by which to remember me and 13s 4d bequeathed to the master, wardens & brothers of the art of Barbers of London for education and meetings.

I bequeath to my daughter Agnes with the permission of the abbess, my tapestry of the Virgin Mary, and request the convent should pray for my soul and also include my former wife, Alice in their prayers,

I bequest to my daughter Mercy the sum of one pound.

The remainder of all my assets, including my monies, my house with its plates, tapestries, and other hangings I bequeath to the Temple Church in Holborn, with a request that they should say prayers for my soul three times a week for three years.

I request that my service to the house of York should be carved on my tomb stone at the Holy Trinity priory at Aldgate as follows: Hic jacet Willelmus Hobbys quondam medicus et cirurgicus illustrissimi domini Ducis Eboric[ensis] et filiorum suorum Regum Illustrissimorum Edwardi quarti et Ricardi tercij quorum anime et animabus propicietur deus amen.

And, my dear fellow, since your Latin is not as good as mine that translates as; Here lies William Hobbys formerly doctor and surgeon of the most illustrious Duke of York and of his sons the most illustrious kings Edward IV and Richard III whose soul and souls God assoil, Amen.'

Amen

# BUCKINGHAM PALACE, A YEAR
# AFTER THE PREVIOUS VISIT

Drs Crick and Hobbys-Pole were ushered into the King's Room again, where they bowed to the monarch, who greeted them, 'Congratulations, I hear you are now married, and are expecting your first child. He or she will bear a hereditary responsibility, a bit like being a Prince of Wales with no choice of your future career. The poor little chap will be expected to be an eminent physician with its awesome medical pedigree. Since your last visit I have visited the Richard III museum in Leicester, poor man he suffered some horrendous injuries, though the worst were struck from behind, while he was defending his front. He may well have struck down Henry VII had he not been betrayed by Stanley, or at least had a few more minutes unassailed from the side, and history would have been so different. His spinal scoliosis looks awful, I see popular belief now is that he may have had little disability in his life, but that had he survived another decade, he would almost certainly have developed increasing back pain and breathless. Richard may well have preferred a warrior's death than physical incapacity, he was such an active vigorous man.'

The monarch accepted some documents from Dr Crick and continued, 'Modern evidence is suggesting that the Tudors, starting with Margaret Beaufort, so beloved by the BBC in the past, were involved in many more nefarious activities than Richard III. That medieval statement quoted by Thomas Hardy, *take have and keep are pleasant words*, is said to have been one of Margaret Beaufort's assertions. It was said about an

American presidential candidate early this century, *time wounds all heels.* Perhaps Margaret Beaufort is about to be wounded. Has your research discovered anything as astonishing as finding that the two princes in the tower were actually female?"

Dr Hobbys-Pole answered, now she had a more important and publically recognised role in their partnership, 'Your majesty, we have some more amazing findings, again for your ears first. We appreciate your royal approval of testing those who are not lineal predecessors of the kings and queens of England. Firstly, Edward of Lancaster, the son of Margaret of Anjou, who died at the battle of Tewksbury, was the son of Edmund Beaufort, the third Duke of Somerset, not Henry VI, a possibility in common credence. Secondly we finally traced the coffin of Perkin Warbeck. His DNA is slightly different from that of Richard III, it is almost certain he was not Richard the Duke of York, but could have been a relative, perhaps an illegitimate son of one of the Yorkist family. Strangely in the coffin we found Richard III's missing second book of hours, dedicated to Edward of Middleham, his son. Warbeck must have had some association with Richard to have that in his possession. One of those involved in his burial would have slipped that in unnoticed by the Tudor officials involved in his execution and burial aware of the considerable personal risk. Warbeck must have been an important person in the Yorkist plans to restore the Plantagenet's to the throne.'

Thirdly, quite astonishingly, we believe we have found Richard, the young Duke of York. It had rumoured that Dr John Clements, an early president of the college of physicians, could have been Richard of Shrewsbury. Clement's early life remains a complete unknown mystery, and Richard was rumoured to have preferred the option of being a Doctor Hobbys II than a King Richard IV. Our archaeologists found Clement's tomb, and amazingly that DNA was almost a perfect match to that of Richard III, he would have been a very close relative, probably his nephew. Checking the DNA of his mother and father would clarify Clement's parentage, but I know you feel very unhappy about doing that. Also in his coffin we found a gold pendant engraved on one side with the boar of Gloucester, and on the other side with a rose, and the serpent and staff of Aesculapius! That finding supports the DNA finding, perhaps Gloucester gave the pendant engraved on one side and Clements added the other emblems. The Duke of York must have been secreted away somewhere for a decade, to return with an assumed identity and live the remainder of his life as a leading physician.'

The monarch looked increasingly astounded by these revelations, but felt they were sufficiently removed from his status as not to undermine his throne. Privately the sovereign was pleased to have declined the genetics group the right to check the paternity of John of Gaunt, Edward IV and Queen Victoria. The position as monarch, the occupant of the ancient royal throne of kings, could have seriously questioned by proven false paternity in any one of them, or any others over the last millennium. The importance of the throne, once again of England only, had been undermined enough by the successful votes for independence in Scotland, Wales and Northern Ireland. Scotland and Northern Ireland left the UK shortly after UK left the European Union, to form a very successful loose federation with the Republic of Ireland, known as Gael and together readmitted to the EU. They had proved their big-picture financial engineering and administrative competence with the construction of the Galloway tunnel from Portpatrick to Groomsport, linking Scotland and Ireland, by digging under the Irish Sea and Beaufort's Dyke sea trench, and their sporting prowess by defeating the English rugby and football teams for the last eight years. The English monarch had to defend vigorously what was left for little England!

The monarch said, 'well Dr Hobbys-Pole, you appear to have confirmed your opinion that Richard III was not the villain portrayed by Shakespeare, he clearly was not responsible for the death of one prince, and why would anyone kill only one, while ensuring the other was successfully concealed, perhaps overseas. Anyway it appears from your evidence that Richard, the Duke of York survived with a changed identity. It seems a bit like today's witness protection schemes. Perhaps you were also correct when you wondered if Edward had any serious disease.'

Hobbys-Pole continued, 'also your majesty, you recall that the Middleham Jewel, a pendant once belonging to Queen Anne, was found near Middleham Castle about a hundred years ago. Our archaeological colleagues are conducting a survey there in the remote hope of finding Hobbys diaries near the same spot. They would certainly shed some light on the more mysterious aspects of the time'.

The monarch's secretary poured glasses of sherry for the three of them, Hobbys-Pole declined accepting some royal mineral water from the Bath springs, the site of the old Roman baths. The all sipped thoughtfully, Crick wondering if he would have success obtaining approval to test former monarchs' DNA from the next monarch, the Princess of Cornwall, the new title of the heir to the throne, currently reading medical sciences at Balliol College, Oxford and likely to be more interested in scientific data, should Crick survive the current sovereign, Hobbys-Pole wondering if her child would ever be seen as an alternative claimant to the throne, it was only a few decades since the transfer of the Baronetcy of Pringle of Stichill from the line of a supposed first son to the line of the second son, when DNA testing revealed a Baroness nearly two centuries ago had been unfaithful. If only their team could only access bones of some former monarchs, she thought. The current incumbent, now widely perceived as firmly on the moral high ground, wondered if dipping quills in another's inkwell in one's carefree hedonistic youth could ever haunt one in later life through the unrestricted research of his two guests.

# ABOUT THE AUTHOR

**Peter Stride** is a recently retired consultant physician living in Brisbane. He graduated MB BS from the Middlesex Hospital, London in 1970 and migrated to Australia in 1975. He is a Fellow of the Royal Colleges of Physicians of Australia, Edinburgh and London, and has a higher medical doctorate, D.Med, from the University of Queensland.

History has been a passion since primary school days in the birthplace of Sir Francis Drake and attending the same public school as King Alfred, though some years later. Growing up in England and overseas as a child of a physician in the Royal Navy one is surrounded by living and ancient history on land and at sea. Peter has some hundred publications, some medical, some relating to aspects of the medicine of history, and some political satire in bridge magazines. After thirty-seven years working for Queensland Health and the University of Queensland, he resigned to spend the last five years working as a peripatetic locum physician in every Australian state becoming familiar with the 'outback'.

Peter has been married to Rosemary, a former nurse and English teacher, for fifty three years and enjoys the company of his three children and eight grandchildren who all live nearby. He has published one previous historical fictional novel, 'William Hobbys, the promiscuous king's promiscuous doctor', about a doctor during the Wars of the Roses, and one murder mystery novel set in Scotland, 'The Islands of Death' and appreciates travel, friends, wine and duplicate bridge.